TREACHERY AT SEA

"Finish him, Noel!" Gumbel shouted. "Stick his gizzard!"

Miller stepped back, breathing heavily. He aimed his pistol at Noel with hatred in his eyes. His finger whitened on the trigger. Without thinking, Noel sprang at him and knocked the pistol up just as it went off. The deafening report and the splatter of blood were simultaneous. Miller's face vanished before Noel's horrified eyes, and his blood splashed hot across Noel's chest. The faceless corpse crumpled at his feet.

Noel stepped back, aghast at what he'd done.

"And where is this big hero?" said a voice that Noel knew better than any other. "Where is this captain killer? I want to shake his hand for giving us this fine prize on a platter. Noel? Noel Kedran, come forth!"

Slowly, Noel turned around.

Standing in the center of the deck with a sword in his hand and a plumed hat on his head, his boots planted wide apart as though he owned the world, stood Leon. He was laughing . . .

Ace Books by Sean Dalton

The Time ∞ Trap Series

Operation Starhawks Series

TIME TRAP

PIECES OF EIGHT

SEAN DALTON

ACE BOOKS, NEW YORK

This book is an Ace original edition, and has never been previously published.

PIECES OF EIGHT

An Ace Book / published by arrangement with the author

PRINTING HISTORY
Ace edition / November 1992

All rights reserved.
Copyright © 1992 by Deborah Chester.
Cover art by Glen Orbik.
This book may not be reproduced in whole or in part, by mimeograph or any other means, without permission.
For information address: The Berkley Publishing Group, 200 Madison Avenue, New York, NY 10016.

ISBN: 0-441-66301-X

Ace Books are published by The Berkley Publishing Group, 200 Madison Avenue, New York, New York 10016.
The name "ACE" and the "A" logo are trademarks belonging to Charter Communications, Inc.

PRINTED IN THE UNITED STATES OF AMERICA

10 9 8 7 6 5 4 3 2 1

To Bruce,
with thanks.

CHAPTER 1

Flung heedlessly through time once more, by the malfunction that held him trapped in the past, historian Noel Kedran materialized in the middle of a raging sea battle with his hands locked around his worst enemy's throat.

His own gray eyes glared up at him; his face, like and yet unlike, glowered and snarled curses at him. He felt as though he were fighting himself, and for a second he was disoriented, confused. As though sensing Noel's distraction, Leon Nardek—his twisted, malevolent twin who had been cloned by an error in the time stream and now stayed somehow joined to Noel in his travels—jerked and twisted in Noel's grasp, struggling to break free.

"Let me go!" shouted Leon in the din of shouts and crashing swords. "Damn you! Let me go!"

Noel tightened his grip on Leon's throat with a fury that left him blind to the mayhem raging around them. "Never! I'm putting an end to you once and for all."

Leon spat in his face. Instinctively Noel recoiled, and Leon almost succeeded in squirming free. Noel threw himself bodily across his duplicate, pinning him down and ignoring the blows Leon struck to his head and shoulders before he got both hands around Leon's throat again.

"You won't kill me. You haven't the guts for it," said Leon, gasping now. His eyes held fear, the cornered rat's kind of fear. "You want to reform me, make me like you—"

"Shut up!" Sick disgust and contempt welled up inside Noel.

"You've meddled once too often, caused one too many innocent deaths. Never again."

As he spoke, he bashed Leon's head against the wooden deck. Leon's face twisted with pain. His fingers clawed at Noel's shoulders.

Noel heaved him up to bash him again, but there came the roar of cannon fire. The deck beneath them bucked and shuddered. Flung flat, Noel lost his grip on Leon, who scuttled away on his hands and knees. Noel started after him, but there was another roar, like thunder echoing across the ocean. The deck shuddered again, and Noel fell.

Only then did he truly become aware of his surroundings. The noise itself was deafening: hoarse voices shouted threats and fearful curses; screams of pain and cries for mercy mingled with the boom of cannon fire and the queer whistling sound of flying ammunition.

Nails, bits of chain, and fragments of sharp metal hailed onto the deck near Noel, cutting down a pair of half-naked men fighting with cutlasses. Screaming and bloodied, both men fell.

"Grape shot!" shouted someone. "They're sweeping the deck with grape shot. God preserve us, and somebody spike that nine-pounder!"

The whistling sound came again. Noel ducked instinctively and looked around for cover, but there was none. The deck was flat, without any kind of structure built on it. Most of the men not fighting were huddled up against the curve of the gunwales.

Tall masts towered overhead against the starlit sky. Sails flapped limply from the halyards. Noel could hear an awful groaning noise from stressed timbers; he realized the sound must be coming from the ship itself.

Sails . . . wooden ships . . . men in pigtails and wide canvas trousers . . . Noel tried to make sense of his surroundings. Where on earth was he this time? *When* was he?

White smoke like dense fog choked the scene. Men scampered through it like demons, brandishing swords, pistols, daggers, and torches. Some carried boarding axes. Brilliant flashes of light cut through the darkness momentarily, bringing the simultaneous roar of cannon fire. Something heavy whistled overhead and landed with a splashing thunk in the water on the other side.

The deck beneath Noel's feet heaved and swung, and through the combined stench of blood, gunpowder, tar pitch, and fire, he smelled the dank saltiness of the sea itself.

Despite the danger surrounding him, Noel realized that Leon was confined to this ship the same as he. No matter where Leon hid, there was only a few hundred feet to search. He would find his murdering, cowardly duplicate, and he would finish him.

A shape loomed from the smoke and darkness, and the flat of a cutlass struck Noel down. The stinging slap of steel across his back hurt like blazes, and Noel barely managed to roll in time to avoid another swipe of the weapon.

"What be ye gawkin' at, ye sniveling coward!" roared a voice like gravel. "We've a ship to take, aye, and booty to plunder. Get to yer feet and board that damned merchantman, ye good for nothin' piece of cod fodder! Stand up and fight, or I'll have yer guts for my cummerbund!"

Noel took one look at that fierce, bearded face, a black kerchief tied over the head, a chest as big as a barrel, and booted legs like young tree trunks. The cutlass whistled at him again, and Noel scrambled away.

He ran full-tilt into a cluster of men. One of them grabbed his arm and shoved him roughly forward.

"Where's yer knife, ye knave?"

"Hah! He's goin' to his Maker. Have a dagger, bucko!"

Noel reached gratefully for the weapon, but another man grabbed his wrist and shoved him back.

"He's none of ours! Send him over!"

With shouts they lifted Noel over the gunwales.

For one panicked instant he thought they were throwing him into the water. "Wait!" he said in alarm.

But instead they shoved him out onto the long bowsprit. Noel looked down and saw black ocean heaving between the hulking bodies of the two ships. The view made him dizzy. He clung to the hewn wood and closed his eyes.

"Hah!"

Someone swooped over him from behind, grabbed him by the collar, and dragged him forward. He caught a confused glimpse of bare legs, callused feet, and a gleaming sword tip before he was hurled bodily through a tangle of cut rigging and fell to the deck below.

"Repel new boarders!" shouted a voice bugle-clear.

Musket fire rang out, puffs of smoke dancing in the darkness, and the whippet-fast rattle of lead balls whizzed past Noel's head.

He ducked and pressed himself flat to the deck of the merchant ship, hugging the shadows between the gunwales and the poop cabin. Without a weapon he had no intention of getting caught up in this mess. Worse, now he was on the wrong ship. Somehow he had to get back and find Leon, but he dared not try with musket balls whizzing in all directions. Dying in the past was *not* one of his goals.

But the fighting surged his way, and two men battling to the death pressed close to his hiding place. One of them, silhouetted in the smoke and darkness with a mane of long hair and layers of pale lace at his throat and wrists, tripped over Noel's foot and fell.

His opponent's sword thrust hard, and passed through the man's body and into the deck planking perhaps only an inch away from Noel's thigh. Paralyzed in the shadows, Noel lay frozen beneath the dead man. Then the victor withdrew his blade, and blood spilled hot across Noel's stomach and legs.

Despite himself, Noel could not hold back a gasp. The pirate heard and swung back.

"Eh?" he said. "Are ye still dying, then, ye dandified cockerel?"

He raised his arm to thrust again, a black shape looming against the sky. Frantically, Noel fumbled through the darkness and seized the dead man's sword. He brought it up just in time to counter the blow, and the clang of steel against steel jolted his arm all the way to the elbow.

"Mother of God!" gasped the pirate, stumbling back and crossing himself. "Do the dead fight on?"

Desperate, Noel seized the opportunity and let out a blood-curdling yell. "I want your soul! I'll eat it in hell!"

The pirate staggered back from him and ran. Noel let him go.

In the distance more cannon fire opened up. Noel looked out across the dark water and saw another ship approaching the two locked together in combat. Wreathed in the smoke from her own guns, moonlight shining white upon her billowing sails, she came up fast, gliding over the black waves with a foamy cleaving of water under her bows. White puffs erupted from her fore guns, and more cannonballs whistled by. One of them plunked into the pirate ship with a horrendous crash that sent planks and splinters flying. Men screamed, and a drumroll sounded.

"Disengage! Disengage!"

The pirates withdrew, falling back quickly. Many swarmed the rigging and used ropes to swing across the distance between the two ships. The rest scuttled back across the bowsprit. One man slipped in his hurry and fell screaming into the sea.

Shouting with encouragement, the merchantman's crew swarmed to the gunwales, firing their muskets at the departing pirates.

For an instant Noel thought he saw Leon on the other ship among the men, shouting and waving a sword. Sails were hoisted, flapping wildly, then swelling with wind. The pirate ship slid away, her bowsprit scraping horribly upon the timbers of the ship Noel stood on.

He ran forward, anxious to get back across before he was left behind. But just as he scrambled awkwardly into the tattered remains of the rigging, seeking to climb up to the bowsprit, a hand clutched his shirt from behind and pulled him down.

"No!" said Noel, twisting in his captor's hold.

A club hammered him between his shoulder blades, driving him to his knees. "You'll not escape so easily, you insolent puppy," growled a voice. "You're going to hang for this night's work."

In an instant Noel comprehended the new danger surrounding him. Still on his knees, he turned and slashed with his sword.

His opponent parried and the sword broke. Before Noel could flee, the seaman swung again, jumped back to avoid the blade, then swung with the club.

The club crashed into Noel's temple. For an instant fireworks seemed to explode across the sky. Then all went black.

He awakened to heat and a dazzling expanse of sun-reflected water. His lips were rimmed with the sour remains of vomit. His parched tongue stuck to the roof of his mouth. Groaning faintly, he managed to roll over.

The clank of chains brought him to full consciousness. He stared at the heavy steel shackle on his wrist and tried to recall what had happened. Bits of memory floated his way, but before he could piece them together, water came sluicing over him in a drowning torrent.

Burning with thirst, he opened his mouth to catch some of it, only to spit it out at once. It was seawater, warm and briny. It sloshed across the deck beneath him and went gurgling over the side.

Noel sat up as another blast of water hit him. Choking and sputtering, he slung back his dripping hair and saw that the seamen had turned a pump on him and the other prisoners chained together on the deck.

The man next to him was rawboned and burned dark with sun. One eye was milky white with blindness; the other squinted balefully. Barefooted and clad in a pair of knee breeches and a tattered shirt, he was scarred and filthy. Despite the glower of defiance on his face, however, his hands were clenched until the knuckles showed white.

Overhead, the masts seemed to reach to the blue sky. There wasn't a puff of wind, and the sails hung limp. They floated in place, becalmed or anchored, Noel couldn't tell. Beside them was another ship, a small sloop smartly rigged. The British Union Jack drooped from her mast.

Noel swallowed hard. Pirates, he was thinking rapidly. British ships. That meant mid-seventeeth or early eighteenth century. It was a cruel era of swift punishment and backbreaking labor. Lives were held cheap.

"They're ready, sir!" shouted a voice in a broad British accent.

An officer of the Royal Navy strolled up the line of prisoners. Bewigged and wearing a tall tricorne hat, he glittered with corded gold braid, brass buttons, and a polished sword. Snowy linen ruffles foamed at his wrists and throat. His blue, full-skirted coat reached to his knees, and his stockings were immaculate. As he came closer, Noel could see his face. It was a beaky, angular one, drawn tight and stern. The officer's eyes shifted, studying the prisoners. He whipped a thin rattan cane across the chest and shoulders of any man who didn't instantly rise at his approach.

The one-eyed pirate beside Noel scrambled up well ahead of time, and Noel did the same. When the officer reached Noel, he stopped and stared. He had the fair type of skin that doesn't tan. His nose was sunburned and peeling. His eyes were a pale, colorless blue. They might have been chips of stone, for all the expression they held.

Having been yanked from the New Mexico Territory by a time stream warped out of control, Noel was aware that his clothing of long-sleeved shirt, bandanna, long sturdy trousers, and high-heeled boots was markedly different from anything of this era. He hadn't identified yet what his LOC was disguised as, but he knew it had to be somewhere on his person.

"Name?"

The officer's voice was high-pitched and so clipped Noel almost didn't understand what he'd said.

When he failed to immediately answer, the officer's brows drew together. He slashed Noel's leg viciously with the cane. The sting of the blow made Noel suck in his breath.

"Name?"

"Noel Kedran."

The cane slashed him again. "You will call me sir."

The pulse in Noel's temples began to beat faster. He barely managed to control his temper. "Noel Kedran . . . sir."

"Colonist?"

Noel frowned. "Not exactly. I'm not a—"

The cane struck, and Noel flinched. "I did not ask for a

long-winded explanation. Answer the questions put to you with directness and brevity. Clear?"

Noel dropped his eyes, seething but aware that he had to keep his anger in check. "Yes . . . sir."

The officer walked on, but Noel's desperation was like something writhing in his throat. He couldn't hold it back.

"I'm not a pirate!" he said to the officer's back.

Someone in the line chuckled. The prisoners stirred, rolling their eyes at each other.

The officer glanced back. "That remains to be seen. Show your papers, all of you!"

Of the dozen men chained, only four fumbled out any papers. The one-eyed man next to Noel had a set. Noel eyed them with curiosity and a rising sense of dread, but he couldn't read the blurred writing on the grimy foolscap.

The one-eyed pirate assumed a military stance, squaring his shoulders and tucking in his chin. "Here ye are, sir," he said smartly. "Forced, I was. Made to pirate against me will."

A man in a plain crimson coat and matching breeches joined the officer. Older, he wore a long curly wig that fell to his shoulders and a broad-brimmed hat turned up on one side and pinned with a brooch, cavalier style.

"These men must all hang, Lieutenant Thurston," he said. His voice was a clear tenor that rang out briskly. "They are scurrilous dogs, murderers, and cutthroats. Not a single man among them deserves mercy."

The pirates muttered angrily and shook their chains.

"Shut your traps!" shouted a seaman. Garbed in short wide trousers and a pigtail, he took the greasy papers and handed them to Thurston. While the lieutenant examined the documents, the seaman glowered at the one-eyed pirate. "Navy, were you?"

"Aye!" said the pirate. "Served aboard the *Driscoll* under Captain—"

"Then you're a damned mutineer!" accused the seaman. "I heard the sad tale of that crew, Lieutenant. They hanged the officers, then deserted and joined with those accursed buccaneers down in Jamaica."

The one-eyed man turned pale. "I never did by choice. God's

my witness, sir, there's my paper to prove I was forced. They'd have cut my throat if I hadn't—"

"That will do," said Thurston curtly. He thrust the papers back.

"Lieutenant," said the civilian anxiously, "you must not show leniency. Set an example with these wretches that will give their brothers pause."

"Captain Miller," said Thurston wearily, "we are quite aware that pirate captains will give any cowardly deserter articles of force for protection in case of recapture. These papers mean nothing."

"God's my witness, sir, but I was forced!" cried the one-eyed pirate desperately. He seized Noel's arm. "Ye heard this man say the same. Have pity on us, sir. Have pity!"

Even Noel could see that his pleas hurt his cause more than they helped. Noel gripped his wrist to quieten him, and the lieutenant noticed.

"Are you the leader of these men?"

"What difference does it make?" said Miller before Noel could answer. "Hang them from the yardarm and be done with it."

The lieutenant's thin nostrils flared in distaste. "You may be content to sail along with carrion swinging from your rigging, but I am not. These men will be hanged in Port Royal, with proper sentencing and documentation of their names."

Miller's face turned as crimson as his coat. "I'll not be a party to this unwarranted leniency! In this damned calm we're days yet from Port Royal. What's to be done with these knaves in the meantime? I ask you, sir, do you expect—"

"They will be kept here aboard your ship," said Thurston curtly, "except for three."

"Hah!" snorted the captain. "You'll regret adding any of these filthy dogs to your crew, shorthanded or no."

"You might consider using some of them yourself," replied Thurston. "You're sadly undermanned for a ship of this size, and you've lost a third of your own men."

"Sir, I—"

"You'll keep the prisoners here!" exploded Thurston, raising his voice for the first time. "Try to remember that if it hadn't been for our intervention last night your neck would now be in a pirate's noose and your crew in shackles. Profit is all you can think about, sir, aye, your damned profit. You sail through the most treacherous, pirate-infested waters in this corner of the world without bothering with the expense of a full crew complement or even a ship to guard you. What the devil do you expect but to be set upon?"

Miller spluttered. "I'm grateful of course, but an extra dozen mouths to feed. Consider it! Our supplies are low already."

"We shall send over barrels of water and provisions."

"It's a stupid waste," said Miller scornfully. "Feeding men condemned to die."

The lieutenant's icy expression did not change. "They'll hang in Port Royal according to due process. We are Englishmen, and we uphold the king's law. The French and Spaniards do as they please, but we—"

"And who is to guard these cutthroats? Kindly remember the delicacy of my cargo—"

"I have not forgotten," said Thurston. "Put them below where they can do no harm."

Noel glanced at the grating set into the deck a short distance away. He could smell the stink of bilge and filth wafting up from the bowels of the ship. The last thing he wanted was to be chained down there in the darkness.

"There is no room," said Miller. "The hold is full. More than full."

"Then leave them chained here on deck. As long as they are in irons, they need no guard."

"Lieutenant—"

"That is all," snapped the officer. "I have no time to delay while Lonigan is prowling these waters. Seaman, fall out three men."

The seaman passed down the line, peering into the hostile or pleading faces in turn. He paused in front of Noel.

"You look sturdy enough. How skilled with sails are you?"

Beside him the one-eyed pirate was holding his breath, standing so tensed Noel could feel it. Noel looked at the seaman. "I don't know anything about sailing."

"Go on!" said the seaman in disbelief. "Lazy, that's what you are. Pirates don't keep them as can't handle a ship."

"I told you I'm not a pirate," said Noel clearly. He held back all emotion from his voice and met the man's astonished gaze. He was aware that the lieutenant was frowning at him, but Noel didn't glance Thurston's way. He'd already made an appeal in that direction without luck. "I don't know one end of a sail from another."

"Well, then, are you the cook?"

"No."

The one-eyed pirate hissed with annoyance. "Are ye daft?" he muttered. "This be yer chance, ye booby!"

Noel turned on him. "How long have I been on your ship?"

The pirate blinked. His gaze shifted to the seaman, then back to Noel.

"Well?" demanded Noel. "How long? What's my job?"

"Uh . . ."

"He doesn't know," said Noel to the seaman. "That's because I'm not a member of the crew."

"Yer callin' Natty Gumbel a liar!" yelled the one-eyed pirate. He sprang at Noel, getting his hands on Noel's throat before he was dragged off. "I'll get ye for that. God's my witness, I will!"

The seaman glanced at the lieutenant. "Sir?"

"This is ridiculous," snapped Captain Miller. "The man is lying in an effort to save himself. Surely that's obvious."

"He's the surgeon!" said Natty Gumbel, glaring at Noel. "That's him. The surgeon."

From down the line came a fresh commotion and a brawny man with a full black beard roared, "Hell open its mouth and swallow ye, Natty Gumbel. I be the surgeon! I be!"

"You seem to be a mystery, Kedran," said the lieutenant. "What are you if not a pirate?"

"I'm a historian," said Noel. "My presence among these men is a mistake."

"Aye, but you're with them!" interjected Miller furiously. "That makes you guilty by association."

"Nonsense!" said Noel. "Why don't you calm down and try to think rationally for a change?"

The seaman punched his fist into Noel's stomach, doubling him over. "Watch your tongue, laddie."

"He's with us!" screamed Natty Gumbel. "If we hang, he hangs."

"That man goes over the side if he opens his mouth once more," said Thurston.

Gumbel fell silent at once, but he went on glaring murderously at Noel, mouthing curses and shaking his fist.

"Your guilt or innocence will be decided by Governor Mountleigh at Port Royal," said Thurston. "Seaman, fall out three men. I have not all day to spend on this matter."

"Aye, sir."

The bearded surgeon and two other husky types were unshackled and allowed into the dinghy that pulled away toward the Navy sloop. The lieutenant paced slowly back and forth on deck, waiting until provisions had been brought back for the prisoners. Then he bade a curt farewell to the captain and departed for his own ship.

"Ye fool," muttered Natty Gumbel contemptuously to Noel. "The lieutenant had his eye on ye. Thought ye were well set up. Ye'd have had a chance on his ship, aye, and me with ye. But now we'll be lucky to ever see freedom again."

Noel just looked at him. Gumbel was a weasel, and he had lied to keep Noel a condemned man with the rest of them. Right now, Noel's exasperation was so great it was all he could do not to throttle the man.

Captain Miller approached them. His fleshy face was set with grim purpose. A rugged individual bare to the waist and carrying a multistrand whip known as a cat-o'-nine-tails followed him.

"There will be no trouble from any of you," he said to the prisoners. "The first man to cause a disturbance will be thrown overboard without compunction. Just because you are prisoners does not mean you won't earn your keep. The deck is filthy from blood and gunpowder. It needs swabbing down. Mind you do a proper job of it, or there'll be no evening ration of supper for you. Bosun! Take charge of these men."

Bald and sporting an earring, the bosun glared down the row of prisoners, then pointed at Noel. "Step forward."

Looking at the man with the whip, Noel obeyed.

The bosun unchained him except for the shackles on his ankles. "Got a special job for you," he said with a sly grin. "Them's as has big mouths is them that gets big jobs."

Still grinning, he led Noel over to the side and tied a hemp rope about his middle. The other end was passed through a wooden block and tackle. Noel was handed a pole with a cloth bundled over one end, then two sailors pulled off his boots and threw him overboard.

He hit the water before he hit the end of the rope. The sting of impact nearly stunned the breath from him. He went under, only to bob back up, choking. Before he could orient himself, the rope jerked him up, causing him to slam against the barnacle-encrusted hull.

"Swab the gun ports!" yelled the bosun, leaning over the rail above him. "Mind you work lively or we'll keel-haul you for good measure."

Noel dangled, spinning gently around and around in midair. Every inch of him was streaming water. He still held the pole they'd given him and he stared at it doubtfully. They had to be kidding.

But it seemed they weren't. A port popped open, nearly whacking him in the process, and a wizened face black with gunpowder peered out at him from the darkness within the ship.

"Howdy!"

The rope tightened around him. Noel could feel it catching him too hard under his rib cage. "Hello," he managed to gasp back.

"Swab lively now," said the gunner. "They'll dunk ye in between ports to wet your rag so hold yer breath when ye've the chance."

"Gee, thanks," said Noel sarcastically. "Couldn't I just dip the end in?"

The gunner cackled. "Ho, that's a good 'un. Where's the

fun, then, eh? Oh, and if ye see sharks, yell out."

"Sharks!" said Noel in alarm. "But—"

"Hop to it! We ain't got all day!"

"Lazy, is he?" called the bosun from topside. "Give him a dunk, Mort!"

"No!" said Noel. "Wait—"

He crashed into the water and plunged under, getting knocked and scraped against razor-sharp barnacles as he was dragged out. They hauled him up even with the gun ports, and he clung to the hull to stop himself from spinning. The rope was cutting him in half and he felt as though he'd swallowed half of the Caribbean.

"Get to work," said the gunner.

Noel did.

CHAPTER 2

That night, a bruised, weary Noel lay on the hard deck, listening to his companions snore beneath a glittering array of constellations in the black sky. The ship dipped and surged steadily, the warm evening breeze filling her canvas. She creaked and groaned and gurgled in a rhythm of rope and timber. The waves chuckled quietly beneath her bows. From down in the hold came the ghostly refrains of an eerie tribal chant. The helmsman stood at the ship's wheel, his shadowy silhouette spinning the chest-high circle of wood with easy competence. He kept his head tilted back to watch the stars by which he set his course. The night watchman paced quietly by and spoke a moment to the guards standing over the prisoners, then walked on.

Curled up with his shoulder wedged against a barrel of coiled rope, Noel fretted with the need to consult his LOC. There hadn't been a chance all day, and he was worried by the amount of salt water the computer had been subjected to. Granted, it was sealed to protect it from the elements, but he wasn't sure it had been designed to withstand frequent and prolonged immersion in the ocean. As for his own status, his throat and nostrils still burned from the quantity of salt water he'd inhaled or swallowed. His clothes were shredded tatters. His hands ached from cuts and splinters.

He was too tired to sleep. So far he hadn't fallen prey to seasickness, but the dip and rise, dip and rise of the ship worried him just the same.

The funeral service for the dead members of the crew had been conducted at midday, giving Noel a much-needed respite from his work. Six bodies sewn into shrouds made from sails, with a cannonball tucked inside at their feet, had been dropped into the water while a drum rolled mournfully and Captain Miller conducted the prayers.

His formal speech had given Noel the date, June 14, 1697. But so far Noel hadn't been able to access his LOC to find out more. He wore a broad leather band stitched together around his left wrist. In his previous travel to the New Mexico of 1887, his LOC had disguised itself as a band of Indian silver and turquoise. In the travel before that to fourteenth-century Greece, the LOC had appeared as a plain copper bracelet. Possessing the capability of molecular shift, it was programmed to alter its appearance to fit the local costumes. And although its damaged circuits kept him from being able to travel back to his own time of the twenty-sixth century, it was still something he could talk to, a piece of home.

It could tell him where to find Leon, now sailing to God knew where on that pirate vessel. Noel was certain Leon was being treated like one of the gang. If there was a band of cutthroats in the vicinity, Leon was always certain to be among their number. Noel hoped that he was finally free of his troublesome duplicate. Maybe Leon's path would never cross his again.

But Noel could not believe that. Ever since he became trapped in the past and Leon had been duplicated by an error in the time stream, he and Leon had been in constant conflict. Leon sought to alter events whenever he could. He wanted to change history and destroy the future that Noel called home. Noel was certain Leon would return to cause more trouble.

The sound of voices roused Noel from his thoughts. He propped himself up on one elbow and saw a woman in a cloak talking to the night watchman.

"Please," Noel heard her say. "I must have some fresh air. I promise I shall cause no trouble."

"Very well, ma'am. But mind ye stay far away from them scurvy prisoners."

She bowed her head, and he let her walk on. Noel watched her stroll the length of the ship on the opposite side. The wind swept her cloak out behind her and now and then a beam of moonlight shimmered on the fine satin of her long gown.

The steadiness of her walk spoke of long days at sea. The tilt of her chin told of courage and determination. He wished he could see her face clearly, but she was only a shadow in the darkness, too far away even for him to smell her perfume.

He had discovered during the course of the day that the *Plentitude* carried a cargo of slaves, silk and other woven cloth, nails, and French brandy in addition to the furniture ordered by the wife of Jamaica's new governor and twenty-two barrels packed with straw to hold her sets of china. The lady herself was aboard, traveling with her cousin, child, and personal servants.

He wondered now if this was the governor's wife or her cousin.

She paused and turned to face his direction as though she sensed his thoughts included her. For a long while she stood motionless, her back to the sea, then she came toward him.

Surprised, Noel sat up, then got to his feet. She stopped well beyond his reach. The moonlight played a variety of shadows across her face. He could tell now that she was young and beautiful. She wore her hair pinned up in clusters of long ringlets. Her gown was cut low and square across the bosom, fitted at the waist, and puffed out in full skirts that went down to the deck. She smelled of ambergris. Diamonds glittered in her ears.

"Are you the man who was found near Lord Davenport?"

Her voice was a warm, melodious contralto. She spoke softly, and when the watchman approached her she lifted her hand imperiously to hold him at bay.

Noel watched her warily. "I don't know."

She pointed to the part of the ship where Noel had hidden last night during the battle. He remembered the gentleman in lace fighting for his life. That man might have been alive now if he hadn't tripped over Noel's foot. Noel swallowed. He had no intention of telling this woman about that.

"You were captured near his body. I think you killed him."

Noel frowned. Captain Miller was still panting for an excuse to hang someone. If this lady started making accusations, Noel's neck would be stretched faster than he could jump overboard.

"Now look," he started, but the watchman stepped forward.

"Mind yer tongue! Show some respect to Lady Pamela."

Noel struggled a moment and managed to control his temper. "I didn't kill anyone last night. It was someone else."

"Easy to say," said the watchman with a snort.

"Please," said Lady Pamela impatiently. "Let me question him."

"It was someone else," said Noel again.

"You saw it happen?" she asked and only the extreme quietness of her tone gave her emotions away.

"He was fighting well, then he tripped. He fell next to me, and before he could recover, the pirate—er—finished him."

Noel frowned, thinking of how close that sword thrust had come to impaling his own body beneath Davenport's. He felt again the hot splash of blood, inhaled again its sickening smell.

She said, "Will you tell me the killer's name?"

"I would if I knew it," said Noel.

She drew in her breath audibly, angered.

"I honestly don't know," he said, wishing she would believe him.

Shaking her head, she turned away. He realized that she might help free him if he could be useful to her.

"Lady Pamela," he said urgently, barely remembering to keep his voice low. "Wait—"

"Leave her be," growled the watchman.

But she stopped and half turned back. Noel said quickly, "I can help you find him. I can lead you to the pirate ship."

She hesitated, the moonlight gleaming silver on her hair, then she bowed her head and walked away. The watchman gave Noel a shove.

"Lie down and make yerself quiet," he said. "I want no more from ye the rest of the night. And don't be putting ideas in yer head, neither."

Frustrated, Noel obeyed. The watchman moved away on his rounds. The muted sound of the ship's bell chimed the hour. Noel sighed. He'd had a chance and he'd blown it. He might not get another. Meanwhile, Leon was free and far away. It wasn't fair.

Natty Gumbel's ragged snoring abruptly stopped. His hand seized Noel's ankle. Noel's heart jumped into his throat.

"No one betrays the Brotherhood, lad," whispered Gumbel. "We'll get ye if ye try it. Fer the rest of yer days, ye'll be a marked man. Fer the rest of yer days, ye'll wonder when it's goin' ter happen . . . a knife in the ribs, poison in yer ale, a carriage runnin' yer down in the streets. Think about it a long time, matey, afore ye decide to do us wrong."

Noel lay frozen, realizing the pirate had been shamming sleep all along. After a few seconds Gumbel released his ankle and resumed his snoring, but Noel lay tensed and uneasy. He believed Gumbel's threat. Through the ages, prison inmates had clung together in cliques and found numerous ways to kill informers despite a lack of weapons and the constant presence of guards. This situation was no different.

He'd accomplished nothing with the woman, and he'd turned the pirates against him.

"Good going, Noel," he whispered to himself and could not sleep.

The next day, Captain Miller put half of them to cleaning brass and mending sails, and the rest went down into the bilge to man the pumps. Noel found himself among the latter delegation.

The hold was a hellish place of dark filth. Groaning slaves lay chained together, packed in so closely they could barely move. Most of them were clad in loincloths and some still wore amulets of bone or necklaces made from animal teeth and shells. They shrank in fear from the lantern light cast across them; their dark eyes held bewilderment and desperation that haunted Noel. He realized that they had been captured from their African villages, rounded up and sold like animals. They did not know the language of their captors. They probably could not envision the grim future that awaited them beyond the slave block.

The bosun shoved Noel forward so hard he nearly stumbled. His ankle chains clanked dismally.

"Get on there! No gawking."

Squeaking rats fled the intrusion of light down into the creaking bowels of the ship. Her timbers stank of damp mildew. The change in temperature told Noel that they were below the waterline now. He thought about those crude wooden boards holding back endless gallons of water, and felt increasingly apprehensive.

Wooden barrels of cargo stood lashed together to keep them from shifting. Crates stamped with exotic trademarks of foreign companies and sacks of grain and provisions filled the space with only a narrow trail leading to the stern.

There, where the ship's hull curved in and the low ceiling kept Noel and his companions from standing upright, the bosun raised a metal grille set into the planking and shone his lantern down into a cavity. Greasy black water reflected the light.

"Down you go," said the bosun.

Noel shivered. He hated cramped, dark places. He hated cramped, dark, *wet* places. The entire hold stank of human waste, rats, rotten grain, and mold, but he had never smelled anything quite as vile as bilge water.

He had never been obliged to stand in any, either. It was waist-high, and that alarmed him more than anything else.

"Are we sinking?" he asked. "Why is there so much water in here?"

The pirates looked at each other, then burst into uproarious laughter. They slapped each other on the shoulders. They shook their heads. They hooted and wiped their streaming eyes. Even the bosun smiled, staring at Noel as though he couldn't believe what he'd heard.

"Aye, you've told the truth," he said. "You're no pirate. You're certainly no seaman."

"That's right," said Noel fiercely, feeling the heat of embarrassment creep past his collar. "I told your captain I'm a historian. He didn't believe me."

"Merciful heavens, are we sinking?" shrilled a thin pirate with buck teeth and a boil-infested neck. He clasped his hands beneath his chin and batted his eyes. "There's water in the ship. Oh, I'm so afraid."

The pirates went off into fresh laughter, while Noel longed to shove the buck-toothed one under the water.

"Enough of your fooling about," said the bosun. "Get to the pumps, and be lively about it."

There were three pumps, odd-looking devices of wood and metal with a double handle on the top that went up and down in a seesawing motion. Two prisoners manned each pump, and a seaman who looked about sixteen squatted above them to hold the lantern steady and to count time.

Every half hour, the boy let them rest while he sounded the bottom with a lead and measured the dropping depth of the water. When the depth was below Noel's knees, the bosun came and escorted them topside again. Noel wanted to ask why they didn't pump out all the water, but this time he held his tongue. Chance remarks regarding ballast and the ship's trim told him enough. By the standards of his own century, the technology of this ship was crude, even primitive, but it worked. The men who operated the ship did so with skill and artistry. Only the harsh conditions and flogging scars on the back of almost every man aboard spoke of the brutality that was commonplace.

Drawing in a clean breath of sea air, Noel paused a moment to savor the sunshine. A small cluster of passengers, including the woman he'd spoken to briefly last night and a young boy with long golden ringlets and a sash, stood at the base of the poop deck.

Noel stared at the young woman in an effort to catch her eye. She refused to look in his direction, however. While she spoke to her companion, her gestures were graceful and animated. Her hair was a lustrous shade of brown, and her skin as pale as cream. She wore a pert straw hat tied under her chin with broad green ribbons, and a long dress of green and yellow stripes. Neither she nor the other woman ventured beyond the shade cast by the poop.

The *Plentitude* was running under full sail, streaming along at a speed Noel found exhilarating.

"How fast?" called the captain through his bullhorn.

An officer consulted a seaman in the bows and shouted back, "Seven, almost eight knots."

"Crowd on more sail!" said Miller. "I want no less than nine knots while we have this wind. If God is with us, we'll make Port Royal by tomorrow."

The order was passed, and sailors scrambled up ratlines into the rigging. Although the mainmast towered almost thirty feet into the sky, the men on the spars seemed unafraid of the height. Some of them even ran along the yardarm without bothering to keep a handhold. Another sail came crashing down, unfurling white and square. Almost at once it swelled with wind, dragging the men below who struggled to belay it.

Noel clung to the railing in delight, letting the wind fling his hair back from his face. He had learned the trick of balancing himself against the pitch and yaw of the deck. In effect, he had found his sea legs. "This is great!" he said.

"Great, is it?" sneered Natty Gumbel, appearing at his shoulder like an obnoxious gadfly. "We'll only reach Jamaica that much sooner, ye fool. Are ye so eager to hang, then?"

Before Noel could answer, a man on the mast yelled, "Sail, ho! Starboard side."

Tension flashed through the crew. The women stopped talking. Even the prisoners ceased working and looked up. Captain Miller, his long wig hanging to his shoulders, strode to the right side of the ship and trained his spyglass on the horizon.

"What's she rigged for?" he asked.

The man aloft stared a long time. Noel himself could see nothing more than a speck of white between the azure of the sea and the paler blue of the sky. The lookout must have the vision of an eagle.

He called down, "Brigantine-rigged, sir!"

Dread flashed across the crew's faces, and the pirates lifted a cheer.

At once Captain Miller whirled around. "Quiet those men."

The bosun laid on the lash, and the pirates crowded back against the railing with reluctance. But they kept grinning at each other, and Natty Gumbel started rattling his chains slyly.

"What's a brigantine?" asked Noel quietly.

Gumbel rolled his good eye while the blind one stared off at nothing at all. "One of ours, lad. One of ours."

The unease on the deck was palpable. Some of the crew shook their heads. The passengers huddled together. Captain Miller's back looked stiff and unnaturally straight.

He glanced up at the lookout. "Is she clean-tailored?"

Again there was a long pause before the man answered: "The sun's in me eyes a bit. Don't appear to be no deckhouses on her, though."

The pirates flashed each other looks of glee.

"It's Lonigan come back to get us," said one.

"Naw, he's gone like a whipped dog," said another. "He don't care about us, nor this plunder. Five pieces of eight says it's Kidd."

"Yer wrong, yer wrong," chanted Natty Gumbel, dancing a hornpipe. "It's Lonigan."

"Naw, it ain't. Ye be daft, Natty, daft in yer pate. Lonigan's heading for the Carolina coast where the pickings are easy. It's Kidd."

Gumbel hooted. "And him in the Red Sea? Get on! Lonigan ain't forgot us. And he don't like to lose. He's been biding his time, waiting to strike again."

The speck of white on the horizon grew larger.

"What flag, sir?" asked the bosun. His bald head gleamed brown in the sun.

The captain kept his spyglass trained on the approaching vessel. "British."

"Thank God," said one of the women.

The pirates snickered among themselves. Noel eyed them with a frown. They were like psychotic children, sullen and vicious one moment, gleeful imps the next.

"Hasn't she seen us?" asked the quartermaster in puzzlement. "She ought to be a trifle more cautious in these waters. Unless she's Navy. Do you suppose Lieutenant Thurston sent her out to protect us?"

Captain Miller watched through his spyglass and made no answer. Then he stepped jerkily back from the rail as though he'd been shoved. He lowered the spyglass to his side.

"She's sent up a Jolly Roger," he said in a hollow voice.

The pirates cheered again, and this time no one stopped them. "Join us, mates!" Natty Gumbel called to the crew. "Surrender this ship to the brethren, and share in the booty."

The bosun struck him with the cat, and Natty squawled in pain.

"Beat to quarters," snapped Miller. "Chain the prisoners to the gunwales. They'll block the attackers' line of fire. Passengers are to get below decks. Bring me the charts of these waters. If we can outrun them, we have a chance of hiding among the smaller islands."

"Sir, we can't outrun—"

"Against a sloop we wouldn't have a prayer, but that brigantine is our size and no faster."

"But, sir, she's gaining—"

"Damn you, man! Fetch me the charts."

"Aye, aye, sir."

The officers scattered to carry out orders. The seamen climbed into the rigging. Atop the quarterdeck, the helmsman grimly changed places with an elderly replacement who was wizened by years spent in sun and salt water. With a cold corncob pipe stuck in his toothless mouth, the new helmsman took hold of the enormous wheel the way a man fondles his wife's breast. The *Plentitude* bore away gracefully and turned her ample stern to the pirate ship.

Her sails filled, then luffed as they turned into the wind. Corrections were bawled out. The crew scrambled rapidly to close-haul the sheets. They tacked across the wind and came on their new course. The sails caught, and the *Plentitude* surged forward. A few minutes later the ship tacked again. Her speed increased steadily, and for the first time since she'd been sighted the pursuer failed to gain on them.

Meanwhile, the prisoners were herded to the starboard side and lined up along the gunwales. A guard held a musket trained on them while a man in a leather apron strung a heavy chain through each man's leg shackles. The pirates were white-faced and fearful. They knew, as did Noel, that they would be cannon fodder in the opening salvo. And if this ship sank, they would sink with her.

Fear was a stink in the air. Below decks the gun ports opened and the cannons rolled into position with a rumble that made the deck vibrate beneath Noel's bare feet.

His pulse hammered hard in his throat. He did not intend to stand here tamely and be chained like a dog, but it would happen unless he could think of a way out. The docility of the pirates surprised him. But without a leader, they seemed incapable of rebelling on their own.

Without access to his LOC, he did not know if this ship was destined to escape or founder. He wasn't supposed to interfere or participate, for he could destroy the future with a single decision. Yet he had to act.

The locksmith was threading the chain between Gumbel's ankles. Gumbel watched with an expression of sick horror, but did nothing.

Noel stared at the pirate ship. It was gaining again, close enough now that he could see her lines. She was long and wide in the beam, and shallow-bottomed to allow her to maneuver easily both in shoal water and narrow inlets. That alone made Miller's desperate plan to hide in some island channel both foolhardy and futile. Two-masted, with a triangular-shaped sail in the stern and two square sails in the bows, the pirate vessel was painted black. Her figurehead was a woman with arms outstretched and hair streaming in thick black coils. One wooden hand held a severed head, and only then did Noel squint and realize that she had snakes for hair.

"It's our *Medusa*!" cried one of the pirates.

Natty Gumbel threw his cap in the air. "Didn't I say it? God's my witness, didn't I say it would be Lonigan's ship? Aye, Black Lonigan, the devil incarnate." He grinned at the crew. "Say yer prayers, mates, fer he'll send yer souls to hell this day."

About that time the *Medusa* ran up a crimson flag beneath her skull and crossbones. The locksmith stared, forgetting his job, and the guard moaned softly.

"They mean to have our blood," he whispered.

"Not mine," said Noel, making up his mind. He shoved past the locksmith and tackled the guard.

The musket went off between them, making Noel's head ring, but the shot went wide and ripped a hole in a nearby sail. At once the wind caught the small tear and ripped it wider. In minutes it was flapping tatters, and the shout went out for a spare.

Noel rolled with the guard, wrenching the weapon from his fingers. Aware that the weapon was spent, Noel swung it like a club and knocked the man unconscious. With howls, the pirates overcame the locksmith and hurled him overboard. Freeing themselves from the long chain, they scattered as rapidly as their shackles would allow.

A pistol shot rang out, and the ball plucked at Noel's sleeve. Whirling, he saw Captain Miller raise another pistol and aim it at him. Noel dived for the deck, and the second shot missed him, grooving into the gunwale instead.

The *Medusa* opened fire with her fore guns, sweeping the deck with vicious chain shot. A second salvo sent bits of metal and scrap iron into the rigging, cutting it and the sails. The *Plentitude* faltered and slowed.

"Break out muskets!" shouted Miller, but by then most of his crew were too paralyzed with fear to obey.

Natty Gumbel struck the *Plentitude*'s colors, and with a roaring cheer, hundreds of pirates suddenly sprang into view from their hiding places on the *Medusa*'s deck.

"Fight to the death, men!" shouted Captain Miller, working frantically to reload his pistols. "It's our only chance."

"Ho the *Plentitude*!" came a shout echoing across the water. "Do you surrender?"

"Get our flag back up, damn you!" snarled Miller to one of his men. The bosun tried to obey, and one of the pirates plunged a dagger into his stomach.

In a mob, the freed prisoners—some armed with knives taken off the crew, others carrying belaying pins—swarmed the quarterdeck, Noel among them. White-faced, Miller and the helmsman backed up.

"Give Lonigan quarter," said Natty Gumbel.

"Never," whispered Miller.

"Sir, it's our life if we don't," said the helmsman.

"I tell you never! It's my ship. I won't surrender her to a pack of cutthroats."

The helmsman spat out his pipe and darted forward. "I'll join with ye. I'll—"

A pistol roar cut him off. The seamed, withered face assumed an expression of astonishment; the squinty eyes opened wide. Without another word, the helmsman crumpled to the deck, his back bloody from where he'd been shot.

Miller threw the smoking pistol aside and raised his spare. Noel saw the defeat in his eyes. He saw the pistol point upward and knew that Miller meant to use it on himself. Outraged by the senseless murder that had just been committed and horrified that the man meant to take a coward's way out and splatter his brains across the deck, Noel jumped forward and grabbed his wrist.

"Don't be a fool!" he said angrily. "You can't—"

Crimson filled Miller's plump face. Enraged, he swore at Noel and struggled to break free of his hold. Aware of the dangerous pistol wavering between them with Miller's finger still on the trigger, Noel strained to lift Miller's wrist. The muzzle swung Noel's way. Gasping, he shoved it back. Around them the pirates shouted and whistled encouragement.

Miller's free fist smashed into Noel's face without warning, just below the painful bruise already on his temple. Jagged pain flashed through Noel's head. He slipped, fighting off the black suction of unconsciousness. Somehow he kept his hold on Miller's other wrist. Miller struck him in the mouth.

Noel tasted blood, and lost his temper. After all, he was only trying to save the stupid fool. He kicked Miller's feet out from under him. The captain fell heavily, dislodging his wig in the process and revealing a pale shaved head. But he didn't drop the pistol.

"Damn you," he gasped. "Damn you!"

He staggered upright, fending Noel off wildly when Noel reached again for the pistol. At Noel's back the pirates waited like wolves circling for the kill.

"Finish him, Noel!" Gumbel shouted. "Stick his gizzard!"

Miller stepped back, breathing heavily. He aimed his pistol at Noel with hatred in his eyes. His finger whitened on the trigger. Without thinking, Noel sprang at him and knocked the pistol up just as it went off. He meant only to point it at the sky, but his shove was too hard and instead he drove the muzzle against Miller's chin. The deafening report and the splatter of blood were simultaneous. Miller's face vanished before Noel's horrified eyes, and his blood splashed hot across Noel's chest.

That terrible instant seemed to last an eternity, then at last Noel forced his nerveless fingers to release their hold on Miller's wrist. The faceless corpse crumpled at his feet, and the spent pistol thudded on the deck.

Noel stepped back numbly, aghast at what he'd done. Around him the pirates were congratulating him and slapping him on the back. The *Medusa* came alongside with grappling hooks and snared the *Plentitude*. While the boarding party swarmed over, Noel wrenched himself free and staggered to the side. He thought he would throw up, but he didn't. Again and again, that scene played through his mind. He felt clammy and diminished. He felt a fool.

"And where is this big hero?" said a voice that Noel knew better than any other. "Where is this captain killer? I want to shake his hand for giving us this fine prize on a platter. Noel? Noel Kedran, come forth!"

Noel closed his eyes, not wanting to believe it yet aware that he'd been expecting nothing less all along. Slowly, still feeling that he would be sick at any moment, he wiped Miller's blood from his face and hands and turned around.

Standing in the center of the deck with a sword in his hand and a plumed hat on his head, his boots planted wide apart as though he owned the world, stood Leon. He was laughing, more alive and confident than Noel had ever seen him; he glowed as though the bloodshed had energized him. For a moment Noel was disoriented. It was like standing in a haze, looking at himself, then the feeling of oneness vanished. They were separate entities again, physical and moral opposites in every way.

Unable to meet those gray eyes that were shaped like his yet of a paler color, like silver, Noel looked down. He saw his hand, bloodstained and covered still with bits of flesh. His hand clenched jerkily, and he brushed his sleeve frantically, slapping it, feeling as though he would never be clean again.

"I don't mind a little blood, brother," said Leon mockingly. "You needn't try to clean up just for me. Come and stand over here. Watch while my men round up the plunder. I'll even see that you get a share for your help today."

Noel glared at him and refused to come any closer. If he'd been able, he would have attacked his duplicate at that moment. His hatred was black in him, growing blacker as though Leon's evil nature was taking root in him.

"Your men?" he managed to say although his voice remained raw. "Since when? How, in the course of two days, have you managed to acquire a ship and crew of your own?"

"Oh, they're not exactly his," said a deep booming voice. The crew parted, and a man strode forward. Dressed all in black from the kerchief tied over his head to his unlaced shirt straining across a massive chest and a pair of leather breeches, he was taller than any other man aboard. A thick black beard covered his face nearly to his eyes. He wore a bandolier with three braces of pistols thrust through it, and was armed with two daggers and a cutlass besides. "I am Black Lonigan, captain of the *Medusa*."

Those of the *Plentitude*'s crew still alive shrank among themselves. Several made furtive signs of the cross.

Lonigan threw back his head and laughed in a rumbling basso. "That's right," he said. "Fear me. Fear my control over your puny lives. I am master of these waters again, and all who sail here belong to me."

Noel managed to regather his wits. The look of admiration on Leon's face was nauseating enough for Noel to speak even more sharply than he intended. "I hope you'll remember that we surrendered this ship to you. You should show mercy now to the crew and passengers."

"Hold your tongue!" said Leon furiously. "You give no orders here."

"Neither do you!" retorted Noel with equal heat. "You may have joined these brigands, but you're still—"

"Silence!" roared Lonigan, making Noel's head ring. He dropped his enormous hand on Leon's shoulder, and Leon stiffened with pride like a dog that's petted. "This man is my quartermaster, so elected by this band. His authority is second only to mine. You will respect that—and him—if you wish to keep your miserable life."

Lonigan stepped away to shout orders at his crew. Noel figured Leon had tampered with Lonigan's mind to become a favorite so quickly.

Leon laughed at Noel. "Not bad, eh, brother? I've finally landed where I really belong." He leaned forward and spat into Noel's face. "In charge of your miserable hide, with the power to let you live or to make you die."

Revulsion quivered inside Noel. He kept his face expressionless, however, and wiped Leon's spittle from his cheek. "If I die," he said softly, "so do you. Don't forget that."

Fear, like a furtive rat, passed through Leon's eyes. Then he sneered. "Before I'm through with you, you'll beg for the mercy of death. You'll beg me!"

"Don't count on it."

Leon stiffened. "Hand it over."

Now it was Noel's turn to feel fear. "Never."

Leon stuck out his hand. "Give it to me, or I swear I'll cut off your hand."

"You can't use the LOC," said Noel, glancing around for a way out, but there wasn't one. "You know that. You've tried it before."

"Neither will you," said Leon.

Only then did Noel understand what he intended. "You can't throw it away!" he said in dismay. "Leon, for God's sake—"

"We are staying here. We are never going through time again," said Leon. He clutched Noel's shirtfront and twisted the cloth until Noel felt the pressure against the base of his throat. "Now hand it over."

"Go to hell."

Leon shoved Noel hard enough to send him sprawling on his back. Before Noel could get up, Leon planted his boot in the center of Noel's chest and aimed a pistol at his hand.

"Remove it, or I'll shoot off your fingers one by one. You can't die from the loss of your fingers, dear brother, but you'll miss them for the rest of your miserable crippled life."

"Leon, *please*."

"Remove it!" shouted Leon. He fired the pistol, and the ball hit the deck next to Noel's thumb.

Noel flinched and jerked up his hand. His heart was thudding violently. His mouth felt so dry it took him several seconds to unstick his tongue.

"You're not that good a shot," he said.

"Tie his hand to the deck!" ordered Leon. "Next time I won't miss. I swear to you I mean what I say."

Noel hesitated, furious at his own cowardice, furious at Leon's irrational demands. More than one of the pirates standing around him had stumps strapped to wooden legs. Some were missing eyes, others hands or arms. This was a world of mutilation and barbarism. He didn't want to join the ranks of cripples.

Besides, the LOC didn't work properly. It couldn't get him home. All it did was jerk him randomly from place to place. Maybe Leon was right. Maybe it was time he accepted his fate and settled somewhere. Keeping the thing wasn't worth this price.

"You're a fool," said Leon, reading refusal into his silence. He raised another pistol.

"Wait!" said Noel, sweating. He struggled with himself, fighting the rising barrier within him. "For God's sake, I—I have the implant. You know I can't just give it to you. I'm *trying*."

Leon eased the hammer down on the pistol. "The implant," he said stupidly. His eyes grew vague as though he was sorting through his own imperfect memory, a memory copied from

Noel's. Then he blinked. "Of course. I'd forgotten."

Wordlessly, fighting the conditioning implanted by the Time Institute to prevent travelers from going rogue and electing to stay in the past, thereby possibly changing the future, Noel held up his left arm. His tattered sleeve fell back to reveal the leather band.

A command from Leon made one of the pirates cut the band off. Noel choked back an involuntary cry of protest.

"It's not even silver," said the pirate in obvious puzzlement. "Why is it worth this struggle?"

Leon looked at the leather strap with revulsion. "Throw it overboard."

The man scratched his head and complied. Noel closed his eyes a moment, struggling to overcome the sense of disaster that gripped him. Now he was indeed trapped in this time. He could never get back.

Never.

CHAPTER 3

Locked inside the captain's cabin with the two women passengers and the child, Noel paced restlessly back and forth across the cramped space. Outside, the pirates had broken into the stores of French brandy and were dancing in celebration while Lonigan and Leon debated over what plunder to take. Because the cabin was located in the poop, a porthole faced the rest of the deck. Each time he glanced outside, Noel could see Black Lonigan lolling at his ease on stacks of coiled rope while the captured crewmen were brought before him one by one. He would hand each man a quill pen. If the man signed the articles, he became a pirate. If he refused, he was shoved aside. All the *Plentitude*'s officers had refused and now stood as prisoners. The first mate was speaking to his companions; presumably he offered them encouragement, but all the men looked afraid.

"What will become of us?" asked Lady Pamela. Her shining brown hair waved softly back from her brow and hung in clusters of ringlets to her shoulders. She sat on the captain's sea chest, having given the one available chair to her cousin, Lady Mountleigh. She kept her cloak wrapped tightly about her person as though she felt cold, but her chin was high and her green eyes flashed angrily at Noel as though she blamed him for what had happened.

"Will you not answer me, sirrah? What will become of us?"

Noel frowned. "I don't know."

"You should know. These are your companions—"

"Pamela," said the older woman in a low voice of rebuke. Plump and pale, she kept touching her bare throat. The pirates had taken her pearls. "Pray hush. These accusations do not advance our cause."

"I shall speak the truth as I see it," said Lady Pamela briskly. She glared at Noel. "I blame you directly for the misfortunes that have befallen us at the hands of these ruffians. You are a murderer and a scoundrel. Not only have you killed my brother, but now poor Captain Miller as well."

Noel's teeth set on edge. "I did not kill your brother! I am not one of these pirates. Why do you suppose I am locked in here?"

"That is a point to your favor," said Lady Mountleigh with a faint smile for Noel. "I am certain my husband will not overlook it when he examines this day's events."

"Rubbish, Caro," said Lady Pamela. "The fellow is a knave. He led the prisoners to revolt and caused our capture. Now he is no doubt placed among us to question and frighten us further." She sniffed. "Well, I am not in the least afraid of you—"

"My name is Noel Kedran."

She ignored his interruption as though he had not spoken. "If you expect us to cower and beg for mercy, you will find yourself sorely disappointed."

The little boy stiffened proudly at her defiant words. He darted at Noel and struck him with a fist. "Take *that,* you scoundrel!" he said and ran back to his horrified mother.

"Neddie, how wicked of you," Lady Mountleigh scolded, hugging him close while he glared at Noel. "You mustn't anger the man, my dear."

"I'll protect you, Mama," Neddie said. "I'm not afraid of these pirates—"

The roar of a cannon made him break off with a squeak. He buried his face in his mother's skirts, and the two women clung to each other.

"What in the name of God is happening now?" asked Lady Mountleigh in a shaking voice. She had turned deathly pale, and her eyes looked enormous with strain.

Noel gazed out the porthole and saw the pirates leaping about the nine-pounder on deck, taking turns loading her and lighting the fuse. The small cannon roared again, belching smoke. Cheers broke out from the pirates, and the musicians from the brigantine resumed playing for the next bout of dancing.

"Don't worry," said Noel. "They're just getting drunk and acting the fool."

"I pray they shan't seek their amusement next at our expense," whispered Lady Mountleigh.

A man screamed, making the women flinch. Noel saw a wriggling seaman hauled aloft by a rope. Some of the pirates stood beneath him and jabbed him with harpoons. Each time he screamed, they roared with laughter.

"What are they doing?" asked Lady Pamela.

She came up behind Noel so quietly he did not hear the rustle of her skirts. Now the sound of her voice made him jump. He turned quickly and put his back to the porthole.

"Stand aside," she said impatiently. "I wish to look out."

At close range, he could see how long and thick her eyelashes were, and how golden flecks danced in her green eyes. Her skin was as delicate and as smooth as porcelain. A small mole at the corner of her mouth fascinated him. She was petite, but shapely, and she carried herself like the queen of the earth. Again he smelled the fragrance of ambergris. Standing there in her satin gown, lace foaming at her bosom and her shape enhanced by corsets, she was the most feminine woman he had ever met.

Her expression, however, was more mulish than sweet. Her eyes, slightly slanted at the outer tips beneath the delicate flare of her brows, fairly snapped at him with annoyance.

"Must you defy me at every turn? Stand aside, I say!"

Noel's urge to protect her from the torture going on outside had been an instinctive one. But her imperious tone drove all thoughts of gallantry from his head. With a glare of his own, he stepped aside and let her look.

The pirates had bound the first mate's arms and feet with rope. They stuck a wad of pitch-coated oakum into the poor wretch's mouth and set fire to it. Within seconds, the man's hair and clothing were also afire. Encased in flames, he jerked and writhed helplessly until Leon took a grappling hook and shoved him overboard.

Inside the cabin there fell a strained silence, broken only by Lady Mountleigh saying, "What happened? Pamela, for God's sake, what are they doing?"

Lady Pamela remained frozen at the porthole, although she no longer gazed out of it. Her eyes were wide, her lips slightly parted. She swallowed convulsively, clenching her fists at her sides. Beside her, Noel wished bitterly that he could have recalled his decision to let her look. He had never imagined they would go that far.

"That man," said Lady Pamela in a low, shaken voice. "Your brother. He is a monster. He . . ."

She did not go on. Noel silently cursed Leon, cursed the circumstances that had created his duplicate, cursed the saboteurs who had tampered with the time stream. Leon was *not* his brother, would never be his brother. And yet, it was impossible to explain otherwise.

"Yes," said Noel resentfully. "Leon."

"He's laughing. How can any of them laugh? How can they do such—"

She broke off and buried her face in her hands. Noel hesitated, then touched her arm. She flinched and jerked up her head, whirling on him with her face white and set. Her mouth was trembling, but her eyes flashed defiance.

"God sees what you do," she said. "God will surely put you in hell for what you do."

Noel dropped his gaze from hers. It would do no good to repeat he was not in league with the pirates. He could not convince her.

The door was unbolted from the outside and flung open. Neddie gasped aloud, and the women clasped hands to give each other courage.

"I pray to God that someone will deliver us," said Lady Mountleigh through trembling lips.

However, Natty Gumbel only gave them a clumsy nod and turned his attention to Noel. "Yer wanted," he said and jerked his thumb over his shoulder.

Noel swallowed and stepped outside. As soon as Natty bolted the door again, Noel said, "What will happen to the women?"

Natty blinked. "Why, nothin', I expect. We got nothin' against women and little babes. It be only their fine pearls and pretty baubles we want."

Following him through the dancing, carousing pirates, Noel let out a sigh of relief. He had not expected men like this to be respectful of women. It seemed inconsistent, but then so far he had found pirates to be completely unpredictable.

"Noel!"

Leon came up to him through the men whirling and dancing hornpipes with such enthusiasm their bare feet thundered on the deck. Grinning hugely, Leon waved a bottle of brandy that looked as though it had been hacked open with a sword instead of being uncorked.

A crash of glass from the stern of the ship and the resultant groan from a knot of waiting men showed Noel that was exactly how they were opening the brandy. A litter of smashed bottles on the deck indicated the number of failures. It was wasteful, but no one seemed to mind.

The men cheered and one danced away with a jagged bottle held aloft. He poured most of the amber contents over his head, then opened his mouth and guzzled greedily without touching the glass to his lips.

"Noel! Brother Noel!" shouted Leon. He threw his arm around Noel and whirled them a couple of times before Noel broke away. "Have some brandy. Join the fun."

As he spoke he shoved his bottle at Noel, who smelled the rich aroma of fine cognac. No one made fine wines and brandies in the twenty-sixth century. That art had been lost—or, rather, thrown away—in favor of synthetic wine. The growing of sun-kissed grapes on sloping hills, the careful measuring of rainfall to determine the sugar content in the slowly ripening clusters, the harvest at exactly the right moment, the wine press, the huge stainless-steel vats and aging casks of oak, the bottling, the tasting, the medals . . . all gone. Instead, men and women drank artificial concoctions that contained no alcoholic quotient, and they depended on their pleasure chips to make them believe they were having a good time. The chips could be programmed with timers; when time was up, the sensation of being drunk vanished. Sober and healthy, the party-goer went home without risk to himself or to others.

Noel was hardly an advocate of drunkenness. But he despaired of the need in his own century for safety above all other factors. No risks; therefore, no need to practice moderation. Substitute reality for fantasy, give up flavor and texture and life for bland banality, and what was gained? Was the quality of life enhanced? He didn't think so.

"Drink, Noel!" said Leon insistently. "Drink, so I can enjoy the taste. Drink, so I can feel what they feel."

Startled, Noel took the bottle and stared at his double. Was it true that Leon was incapable of tasting and experiencing through the physical senses on his own? He knew that Leon felt his pain. Perhaps Leon shared his other emotions as well.

The idea angered Noel. It made him feel invaded, exposed. He looked at Leon with contempt. "Is that all you are, a voyeur?" he asked.

The grin vanished from Leon's face, leaving something humiliated and furious in his eyes. He struck without warning, his fist smashing into Noel's jaw.

Noel went staggering back, bumping into a pair of pirates who cheerfully shoved him toward Leon again. One of them plucked the brandy bottle from Noel's hand and poured the contents down his gullet like water.

Noel raised his fists, but even as he and Leon circled each other, seeking the right moment to attack, the music abruptly stopped. Pirates were shoved aside right and left, then Black Lonigan stood there, towering over all of them, his beard foolishly braided with Lady Mountleigh's pearls.

"There is no fighting among ourselves!" he roared in a voice like thunder. "Leon! You made yourself one of us when you signed the articles. Do you want to lose your share of the plunder for this?"

Leon straightened from his battle crouch and dropped his hands to his sides. "Noel is not one of us," he said sullenly. "Not yet."

Black Lonigan's dark eyes swept to Noel. "But you soon will be, eh, bucko?" he said softly.

Noel hesitated. He did not know which course to take. Without data from his LOC, he could not determine how history was being changed. Yet he had no choice, now, but to carve out a place for himself in this time. Unlike Leon, however, he did not want to spend the rest of his life with thieves and scoundrels.

"Well?" said Lonigan. "Will you go on the account with us?"

"What's going to happen to the women?" asked Noel.

"Noel, don't be a fool," said Leon angrily.

Noel ignored him. "What happens to the women? What happens to the men who refuse to join you? Are you going to kill all of them?"

Lonigan shrugged. His face gave nothing away. He snapped his fingers, and a tall, ebony-skinned man appeared from the crowd. Thin to the point of emaciation, he was so dark he seemed to absorb the light. His teeth were filed to sharp points and stained red, almost as though he'd been eating raw meat before he came aboard. He smelled of death—cold and stale.

He had strange, compelling eyes. Eyes like obsidian. Eyes like a tar pit, dragging Noel down. A haze shimmered around Noel, and all the noises faded. He felt isolated from the men surrounding him as though he stood in a jar and could see them only through the distorted curve of the glass sides. But the black man's eyes stayed with him, holding him mesmerized. He was drawn deeper and deeper, and although inside he knew he should resist, *must* resist, still a curious lassitude possessed him.

In the deepest, farthest reaches of the man's gaze, Noel saw a flame. He felt the heat of it scorch his face. He heard a voice, deep and resonant, vibrate through him.

I am Baba Mondoun, said the voice.

A low moan rose through Noel, although he knew he did not utter it aloud.

I am a Bocor. *I see into men's souls. I know all things through the gifts of the gods. You are mine, Noel Kedran. You are mine. When I call you, you will obey me. Say it.*

The words swelled in Noel's throat. He did not want to speak, yet something seemed to control his body. His lips moved and he whispered, *"Yabo, Baba."*

The flames before him danced brighter. Their illumination grew blinding, all encompassing. Then, abruptly, they vanished. He saw the man blink, and he blinked too. Lonigan turned to shout a command at someone, and Mondoun walked away. Noel felt staggered and without support, as though he might lose his balance. Suddenly he could hear again. Noises assaulted his ears.

Natty Gumbel gripped his wrist. "Ye don't want ter be marooned, now, d'ye? God's my witness, ye can starve quick enough on some of these scrubby sand heaps. There be some without game or water. There be some that disappear at high tide. And where would that put ye but gluggin' in the deep? Ye want none of that, lad. Put aside yer scruples and sign on. Ye'll be a free man and a rich one to boot. Black Lonigan's men never starve. Meself, I'm glad ter be in his band. He'll treat ye better than ye had it before."

Noel looked around and saw Black Lonigan holding out the ink pot and quill pen. A slow smile spread across the pirate captain's face.

Noel shivered. He started to speak, then forgot what he meant to say. Although he had intended to defy Lonigan, he took the pen and signed the articles.

"Do you want a scrip to show you've been forced?" asked Lonigan.

Noel remembered the naval lieutenant's scorn for such documents. "No," he said.

His voice sounded tinny and far away. His skin felt flushed and hot.

"Welcome to the crew of the *Medusa*," said Lonigan. "Leon will award you your share of the plunder."

Lonigan smiled to himself and strode away, shouting orders for the crew to divide itself between the *Plentitude* and the *Medusa*. He wanted to sail both to Tortuga. Although drunk and disorderly, the pirates obeyed, changing out the torn sails and separating the two ships. The *Medusa* took the lead, and the *Plentitude* followed five hundred yards off her port stern, avoiding the brigantine's foamy wake.

Noel's knees felt oddly weak. He sat down on a small keg of rum and wiped his sweating brow. Leon gripped his shoulder, and when Noel glanced up he was surprised to see his duplicate looking pale and shaken.

"What did Mondoun do to you?" demanded Leon in a low voice. "Where did you go?"

"What are you talking about?" said Noel.

"You *left*," insisted Leon. "You stood there right in front of me, but I couldn't sense you at all. You *vanished* from my mind. Now where the hell did you go?"

Noel shook his head. "You've been in the hot sun too long," he said. "I was right here."

"No, you—"

"Drop it!" said Noel irritably. "You're sounding like someone with a bad head chip. Go pester someone else. Flog a few backs. Put on some more sail. Walk the gangplank, but leave me alone."

His head was throbbing. He rubbed his forehead, but that didn't help.

"There is something you are not telling me," said Leon. He shook Noel's shoulder. "I can tell when you're lying! What do you know? What did you do? Is it the LOC?"

Noel slapped his hand away. "The LOC is gone, remember?" he said bitterly. "You threw it overboard."

"Perhaps, and perhaps not. You could have tricked me."

"Search me then."

Leon's eyes narrowed. "Maybe I should. I don't trust you."

Noel shrugged in irritation. "You don't want me aboard. You don't want me dead. You don't want me marooned. Have you ever wondered if there's a consistency problem in that short-wired brain of yours?"

Leon's mouth clamped in a thin line. His eyes blazed. Before he could retort, however, nausea rolled in Noel's stomach.

He jerked himself to the railing and vomited. There was nothing in his stomach to bring up, yet the dry heaves wracked him severely. He had a momentary sensation of something wriggling and furry passing up his throat. Then it was gone, the spasms ended, and he sank to his knees with a sigh of relief.

Already his headache was gone. He no longer felt feverish or weak. It must have been a little Caribbean virus, coming and going. He hoped it was gone.

Brushing his fingertips across his forehead, he found his skin cool and dry. Energy flowed back into him. He got to his feet and glanced at Leon, who stood staring at him in an alarmed manner.

"What's your problem?" asked Noel. "What are you looking at? Ever see *mal de mer* before?"

"You aren't seasick," said Leon, still looking at him with a mixture of puzzlement and fear. "Your eyes—"

"What about my eyes?" snapped Noel.

"They're clear now. A few minutes ago, they looked . . . strange."

"What do you mean, strange?"

Leon shrugged. "Just . . . strange. I don't think I was talking to you."

Noel backed up a step. Leon had always been weird, capable of using ESP and limited forms of mind control on some people. But now he sounded like he had lost his mind.

"Sunstroke is a dangerous thing," said Noel carefully, watching Leon as closely as Leon was watching him. "You didn't do too well in the heat back in New Mexico. Maybe you'd better stay in the shade for a while."

"It's not the sun!" said Leon impatiently. "It's you! Something has happened to you. Or did happen to you. Why do you keep denying it?"

Noel shook his head. "I don't know what you're talking about."

"You just don't want me to know. You always want to keep me out. You and your smug feelings of superiority. Well, remember this, dear brother—"

"I'm not your brother, dammit!" snapped Noel. "Stop calling me that."

Leon glared at him. "You just remember that we're on equal footing now. You don't have the LOC. You're no better than me."

"I'm still real," said Noel softly. "You're not."

Hatred blazed in Leon, and Noel braced himself for an attack. But Leon restrained himself this time. He said, "Consider this for a while. I don't think you're real anymore either. I think you're changing."

"That's impossible!"

Leon smirked. "You sound afraid."

"Don't be ridiculous."

"Changing. Maybe fading."

"It can't happen."

"It might."

"No."

"You've changed already," said Leon. "I can sense it. I can smell it on you, see it in you. I *know*."

"You know zip."

"Then why are you so scared inside, deep inside, where you think I can't see?"

Noel stared at him, confused and annoyed, unable to answer. He knew Leon couldn't read his thoughts. At least Leon never could before. Was it different now?

"Leon," he said uncertainly, but with a scornful shrug Leon walked away.

CHAPTER 4

By evening they dropped anchor in the tiny bay of an uninhabited island. The sails were furled and lookouts posted. Dinghies set to, rowing load after load of men to shore from both ships.

Assigned to help load empty water barrels into the dinghies, Noel paused in his work to look around. The bay, though small, was protected by a curved headland, quite rocky and covered with scrub. Pure white sand glittered on the beach beneath the incoming lap of the tide. The sunset was a brilliant ruby color that turned the water bloodred. To the east, a black bank of clouds had massed with cirrus clouds fanning across the sky. The air was still hot despite the dropping sun, very moist and heavy. The open seas were growing rough, and the barometer was falling. A storm was coming, a bad one from the signs. Some of the pirates watched the sky uneasily. Others, like Leon, ignored the situation.

Monkeys screamed from the branches of graceful palm trees, and birds shrieked and fluttered in alarm as the pirates landed and set up camp. Some of the men went fishing and foraging. Soon a huge turtle was turning on a spit, and fish were wrapped in wet fronds for roasting in hot coals. Lonigan even let the women and the shackled officers of the *Plentitude* come ashore. They were set to gathering coconuts under the watchful eye of their guards. The bosun and ship's carpenter hacked their way into the jungle with their swords and reclaimed a trail leading to fresh water. Using crude wheeled platforms

45

designed to move cannons into position, Noel and a team of pirates filled the water barrels with the cold spring water gushing from a tiny waterfall in the cliff face of the island's central hill, then hauled them back to the beach. Capped with wooden lids, the water barrels stood ready for loading. Fish were salted and packed into provision barrels. Leon killed a wild boar with a musket. The beast was butchered on the spot and salted down too, and Leon was hailed as king of the island.

Lady Pamela was named queen. Brought unwillingly into the pirates' midst, she stood stiff and expressionless while they took turns bowing to her. The firelight reflected off her hair. Her eyes were as intense as emeralds.

The cook brought her the choicest turtle meat, tender and flavorful, sizzling with juices. She looked as though she would refuse, then accepted the offering with a regal nod of her head. Satisfied, the pirates let her return to Lady Mountleigh and the three-sided hut that had been erected for them out of branches and palm fronds. The pirates had also supplied the women with massive chairs of carved oak and a fine Persian carpet that they unrolled over the sand.

Lonigan broke out the rum kegs, and soon the pirates were happily guzzling from their tin mugs and gorging on fish and turtle. The musicians played eerie rhythms and drumbeats that sounded pure African. Occasionally in a break in the general noise, Noel could hear voices chanting from the hold of the *Plentitude* in response. He hoped the poor slaves did not think they had been returned to their own home shores. As far as he could tell, Lonigan intended to sell them on the block in Tortuga for a fine profit. There were black members of the crew who must have been slaves themselves once, yet none of them seemed to identify with the plight of the poor wretches chained in that filthy hold.

Rum flowed freely, and while some of the men danced, others lounged on the sand and spoke of how they would spend their money once they landed in port. The women in Tortuga were the best, Natty Gumbel claimed. Doe-eyed Spanish women with pale skin and tiny waists. Regal mulatto women. Women with skin like black satin, calling out enticements in French. Lush, generous women everywhere, standing on their balconies whenever a ship came in, waving, willing, wonderful.

In the midst of this fantasy, told to the derision of most of the men, Black Lonigan spoke briefly to Leon, then slipped away from the company. Noel saw the captain stride away into the shadowy jungle carrying a heavy sack of swag over his shoulder. He took neither weapon nor a lantern. The moon overhead was obscured by cloud cover, and the amber light from the campfires did not penetrate far into the trees. When Lonigan did not return after several minutes, Noel wondered what he was doing out there alone. Burying treasure?

He joined Leon, who was watching a dice game and scowled at his approach.

"Want to gamble away your share?" Leon asked. He held a rum cup that was nearly full, and although he sipped from it now and then he did not seem to enjoy it.

By contrast, most of his companions had flushed faces. They were beginning to laugh at nothing and everything. They swigged the potent rum as though it were water. Their wagers were reckless. None of them cared whether they won or lost.

"What's Lonigan up to?" asked Noel quietly beneath the noise.

Leon's scowl deepened. "How should I know?"

"He spoke to you before he left."

"I'm the quartermaster," said Leon with a sneer. "You're just one of the crew."

"We're all equal under pirate law," said Noel.

Leon gave him a rude gesture.

"Tell me."

"He's gone to take a bath. Now go away. You're spoiling my game."

Noel walked away from the gamesters. He stared at the jungle, feeling restless and edgy. The rumble of the drums was beginning to throb in his senses. He wished they would fall silent, but no one else seemed to mind them. Rain began to mist lightly, hissing as it fell on the fires. He could hear the wind rustling the palms.

Lady Pamela gestured to him. It was a quick, nervous wave as though she wanted no one but him to notice. Noel dismissed his curiosity about the captain and went to her.

"Is there something I can do for you?" he asked.

The women sat on their chairs with visible tension radiating from their faces. They were sitting as far back under the overhang of their crude shelter as possible, yet the firelight still flickered across their gowns and faces. The boy was curled at his mother's feet, his head leaning against her knee. He had gone to sleep, and Lady Mountleigh's soft plump hand rested protectively upon his small shoulder.

"Please," whispered Lady Pamela. "Those poor men have had no water and no food." As she spoke she gestured at the prisoners, who sat chained to the palm trees like dogs forgotten by their masters. "Will someone not have pity on them?"

Without a word, Noel fetched a water pail and took it to each of the prisoners in turn. "God bless you," whispered one.

Another nodded his thanks, but the majority of them maintained proud silence. Their eyes, reflecting the dancing flames of the campfires, shimmered with contempt. Noel didn't care. He'd been their prisoner first. At least right now, he had a sliver of freedom.

He gave them breadfruit and some mangoes to eat and returned to Lady Pamela.

"Thank you," she said.

"What about you?" he asked. "Did you get enough to eat?"

She glanced away as though her appetite was unimportant. "Please," she said. "It's raining. We should like to retire. When may we return to the ship?"

Noel glanced at the pirates. Some of them had fallen into drunken stupors, lying sprawled like puppies in the sand. Others were singing a sea chanty that had no connection to the drumming. Noel frowned. That drumming was like an itch under his skin. It was driving him crazy.

"I think you are to stay here tonight," he said. "The queen of the island has to stay with her subjects."

"That's ridiculous," she said sharply. "I won't be treated this way—"

"Pamela," said Lady Mountleigh in warning.

Lady Pamela turned crimson. She drew in her breath audibly and held it, fuming. Her fingers made numerous tiny pleats in the lap of her gown, smoothed them out, then made more pleats.

"This is intolerable," she said at last, her voice back under her command. "We cannot sleep here, out in the open like savages, certainly not among these men. It's barbarous."

"They will not harm you," said Noel.

"You may believe that. I do not." She reached out as though she would touch his hand, then curled her fingers into a fist and drew back. "Please take us to the ship."

Sighing, wishing he could help her, Noel started to reply when he heard something. He frowned and turned his head toward the jungle, listening.

It came again, a soft, clear trill of sound, high in register like the notes of a flute, yet delicate without a trace of shrillness. It turned his blood to ice water.

"What is it?" asked Lady Pamela in alarm. "What is out there?"

"Don't you hear it?"

"Hear what? Is it a boar, a wild animal, savages?"

Noel shook his head, listening to the thin piping. It played an odd, disconnected melody that seemed elusively familiar. He was certain he had never heard it before, yet he must have.

"Mr. Kedran—"

Noel stepped away from her, forgetting her as though she'd never existed. He walked away from the dying firelight into the trees. In seconds the darkness swallowed him.

It was like being unconscious and suddenly jerking awake. Startled, Noel stared around him and realized he had no recollection of how he'd come here. He was standing in a small cave, a shallow scoop in the limestone of the hill approximately the size of his office back at the Time Institute. He did not think he'd blacked out. He hadn't opened his eyes. It was as though he'd been blind and now he could see again. He remembered leaving the camp, then nothing until now. Yet he lacked any sense of time having passed.

Still, how he'd gotten here hardly mattered, for it was what he faced that concerned him now.

In the center of the cave, Baba Mondoun sat cross-legged on the ground, naked save for a white loincloth. His black skin glistened as though he'd been oiled. He wore a shoulder-length periwig, white with powder, and a black tricorne hat. Before him glowed a red-orange light, the color of fire, yet no flames crackled. Noel could not see its source. His instincts warned him not to look too closely at that light.

His heart thudded violently. The cave was stifling hot, so hot he could scarcely breathe. He could see ripples of heat in the air, making Mondoun shimmer. Noel tried to step back, but he found his feet rooted to the ground. He could not lift his arms, twitch his fingers, or turn his head. Only his eyes could move. They darted from side to side, seeking a way of escape, but the cave's entrance—and exit—must be behind him, for he could not see it.

He wanted to speak, but he could not. An invisible band constricted his throat. Each time he tried to make a sound, the band tightened. The fear of choking made him give up, frustrated, angry, and frightened. Sweat ran down his face, stinging his eyes. He blinked and wondered what in blazes was going on.

Mondoun seemed oblivious to his presence. The *Bocor* was bent over, his whole attention riveted to his task. In his hand was a white powdery substance that looked like flour. He dribbled it onto the floor in an intricate, scrolling pattern. His skill amazed Noel, for he never faltered, never made a mistake. The pattern taking shape was symmetrical, flawless, yet done entirely freehand.

He finished, returned the unused portion of flour to a small pouch and commenced a second, smaller pattern with a handful of red powder. While drawing this one, he began to chant softly, then to sing in a lilting rhythm that was almost hypnotic. Noel could feel the threads of a pattern running through his mind, as though Mondoun was drawing a *vèvè* in his senses. The song held a mixture of French, English, and island patois. It was also African juju.

Noel realized he was witnessing voodoo, and his blood ran ice-cold.

Part of his training as a historian had been in ancient religions. Because superstitions were not confined to strict chronological periods, but instead reached far beyond their original times, the Time Institute made certain travelers were acquainted with all the major religions and numerous smaller cults. Because he specialized in Roman, Greek, and Egyptian history, Noel knew all about ritual sacrifice. He had participated in the Elysian Mysteries. He had watched temple processions in Thebes. He knew the rites of the dead, and which pantheon of gods preferred which kinds of offerings. Beyond those, however, his knowledge was more general. He had studied the Druids, the medieval convolutions of the Christian church, the cruelties of the Aztecs, and the dark African mysticism that had spread to the rest of the world during the centuries of slave trading.

He did not believe in voodoo. But he did know its followers were capable of slaughtering him as a sacrifice if it fitted their purposes.

It was harder than ever to breathe. His chest felt as though iron weights were pressing it down. Mondoun threw a substance into the source of the weird orange light, and acrid, sour-smelling smoke belched forth. Noel choked on it. He tried to turn his head aside, tried to hold his breath, but it was everywhere, pervading every inch of the cave.

Mondoun breathed deeply, filling his lungs and closing his eyes. Noel's desperate lungs fought his control and grabbed a quick breath. The smoke got to him. He coughed, gulped in more. The top of his skull went numb, and his heart hammered out of control.

He had been implanted with a certain amount of protection against the drugs and potions of antiquity, but this smoke was too powerful. He suspected it was a hallucinogen, but the head trip he feared didn't happen.

Instead, Mondoun opened his eyes and stared directly at Noel. Once again Noel was mesmerized by their dark intensity. He felt unable to look away, yet he didn't want to be hypnotized again. He could hear a roaring in his ears, and the room began to float slightly.

"What is my name?"

"Go to hell—"

The invisible band choked his throat. Noel wheezed for air.

"What is my name?"

The roaring was louder, and behind it Noel heard the crackling sound of flames mingled with wild shrieks and bursts of laughter.

"What is my name?"

"Baba Mondoun," said Noel.

As soon as he said the name, the eerie light in the cave flared more brightly, and the words seemed to echo in his chest with every beat of his heart.

"It is so," said Mondoun. "The world cannot see truth. The world is easily deceived. What am I?"

A tiny corner of Noel's brain fought the spell, yet he said, "You are a *Bocor*, a p-priest of the b-black magic."

"Good. Hear the names of the black gods: Congo Moudongue, Congo Savanna, Congo Maussai. Say the dark names. *Congo*."

"*Congo*," said Noel dully.

"*Pétro.*"

Noel shivered. "*Pétro.*"

"Welcome the Petro Maman Pemba. Welcome Ti Jean Pie Fin. They are the dark angels whose hands are over you. Let them come."

"No," whispered Noel, sweating.

"Let them come."

"N-no."

But he could hear them, despite his feeble denial. Hissings in his ear, streams of words in Swahili and Bantu, faint screams that chilled his blood, icy caresses across his burning skin, the touch of tongues like snake flickers. He shivered, feeling sick.

"You bring us a gift, Noel Kedran," said Mondoun.

"I have nothing."

"It is a great gift, a gift of much power. A gift neither of the *Pétro*, nor of the *Congo*, nor of the white *Rada*. A gift any may use. Bring it to us, Noel Kedran."

At first Noel did not understand, then the memory of Leon throwing the LOC overboard came to him. His anger boiled in his throat.

"LOC," said Mondoun, putting power on the word. "Bring us the LOC."

"C-can't," gasped Noel. "It's gone."

For the first time he was glad. He wasn't sure how any of this was happening, but he knew that it was taking place. This was no dream. In dreams, if you felt frightened enough or sick enough you woke up. He was so scared his heart was trying to pound its way out through his ribs. He felt clammy and hot—icy cold, then burning with fire. But he hadn't awakened. That meant this was real. And he was glad Leon had thrown the LOC into the ocean, glad that a creep like this couldn't get his paws on the device.

Mondoun laughed. It was a deep, rumbling sound like thunder at first, swelling to a great, bursting guffaw. He put his hands on Noel's shoulders, still laughing, his pointed teeth bared in the strange light. His touch melted the paralysis holding Noel a prisoner. Noel gathered himself to run, but he found his strength fading along with the paralysis. It felt as though he were melting in the heat. He looked down at himself, expecting to see his flesh and bones sliding into a puddle of liquid. Before he knew it, he was on the floor, flat on his back, with no more ability to move on his own than he'd had before.

In his mind he raged at this stupid helplessness. He was supposed to know how to avoid hypnotism. He was an educated, sophisticated man of the future, for God's sake. He wasn't supposed to turn into a quivering believer whenever he encountered a cult.

He wasn't supposed to let himself become a victim either, but here he was.

Mondoun produced a dagger, wickedly sharp at the tip. Noel steeled himself, wondering if it was going to be the wrists or the throat. Instead, Mondoun sliced open his shirt with a swift deftness that left not a nick or a scratch on Noel's skin.

Mondoun began to chant, his voice rising and lowering rhythmically until Mondoun himself looked in a trance. Mondoun scooped up a yellow powder that smelled bitter and began to draw a *vèvè* on Noel's chest.

Noel tried breathing harder, hoping the rapid rise and fall of his chest would cause the *Bocor* to make a mistake. He failed. He tried lifting his head and blowing at the powder to spoil the intricate design. That didn't work either.

The hissing noises returned, surrounding him. He felt talons dig into the flesh of his arms, yet he saw nothing but Mondoun working over him. His heart pounded like it was going to shake itself apart. In his mind appeared the image of the LOC, growing more and more vivid, activated so that its clear sides revealed the colorful pulses of its fiber-optic circuitry. Around him the smoke curled and formed, swirling in a myriad of ghostly shapes until it began to resemble the LOC.

Suspended on the wraith tendrils of the smoke, the LOC looked more and more real, as though if he lifted his hand he could pluck it from the air. The last of Noel's resistance crumbled before that image. He longed for it with an intensity that hurt. Although he knew it was damaged beyond repair, although he'd accepted the fact that it could no longer take him home to his own time, nevertheless he needed it for hope, for the courage to go on.

Around him rose shrieks and wails. Mondoun's voice cracked with exhaustion, and abruptly the chanting stopped.

The orange-red light had faded to a muted flicker. The cave smelled of sweat and mice. The heat diminished, and the cooler air made Noel shiver. He realized with a start that he could move.

He shoved himself up onto one elbow and paused as a wave of dizziness swept over him. Putting his hand to his forehead, he slowly sat on up.

Beside him, Mondoun pulled off the ridiculous hat and wig and stared at him.

"Take it," he said. His voice was a whisper of its former resonance. He looked drained, yet triumphant. "It must be your hand."

Noel looked up and saw the hallucination was still spinning in front of him. The LOC, not activated but clearly visible, still floated on a finger of smoke. Noel blinked and rubbed his aching eyes.

"Take it!" rasped Mondoun.

Noel reached out, expecting to see his fingers pass through the vision. Instead they clutched the smooth, cool surface of the LOC. Disbelieving, he grabbed it.

It rested on his palm, real, *there.*

He touched it with his fingertip, prodding it.

It was real.

He grinned. He laughed aloud. "I don't believe this! How did you—Never mind. I don't care. I thought this thing was gone for good."

"Bring it to life," said Mondoun wearily.

"Yeah, I guess I should check it out. The salt water might have damaged it. It's sealed to a depth of one hundred meters, but there's no telling how far it sank."

Even as he fitted it on, Noel's mind was still reeling with amazement at Mondoun's mastery of that much telekinetic energy. He wasn't supposed to activate the LOC in front of anyone, but right now Noel didn't care.

"LOC," he said, his voice unsteady and eager. "Activate."

For a moment nothing happened.

"LOC!" he said sharply. "Activate."

Warmth ran through the bracelet encircling his wrist, warmth like a kiss from an old friend. The LOC hummed to life and flashed on, its circuitry pulsing steadily.

"Working," it replied tonelessly.

Noel couldn't believe it. He laughed, feeling his eyes turn misty. He was so relieved to hear LOC's voice. "Run diagnostic checks. Any water damage?"

"Negative."

He grinned. "I guess you're not such a piece of junk after all."

"Affirmative."

"Run a scan of date and location. We're in 1697, location Caribbean. Specify the history of a ship called the *Plentitude*. Her captain was named Miller. What happened to her crew?"

As he asked the question, Noel's gaze shifted to Mondoun. The man was sitting down, still breathing heavily. It was a good time to make a break, but Noel was no longer afraid.

" . . . working," said the LOC. "*Plentitude* . . . merchant ship under English registry. Tonnage . . ."

"Stop. Skip those statistics. Continue."

The LOC hummed, then resumed. "Foundered in storm. Went down with all hands on June sixteenth, 1697."

"Today is the fifteenth," said Noel.

"June fifteenth, 1697."

Noel whistled soundlessly to himself. From the corner of his eye he saw Mondoun watching, listening. Noel swallowed. "Any survivors?"

"Affirmative."

"Who? Come on!"

"Records are incomplete."

"Is this data within your damaged lobes?"

"Negative."

"Continue. Specify as many survivors as you can."

"Two passengers."

Noel's mind flashed to Lady Pamela.

The LOC pulsed steadily. "Lady Mountleigh, wife of the governor of Jamaica."

"And Lady Pamela Davenport," said Noel.

The LOC was silent for a moment. "Unknown."

Noel frowned. "What do you mean, unknown?"

"Records are incomplete."

"Was the other survivor Neddie or Edward Mountleigh?"

"Unknown. I scan an Edwin Sinclair, later Lord Mountleigh. He dies of smallpox in 1724."

Noel stopped paying attention. He was thinking of beautiful, fiery Lady Pamela drowned. That wasn't fair, wasn't right.

The LOC droned on: "Mountleigh estates in England and Jamaica were entailed. Edwin Sinclair is the last male heir of the family. After his death, the lands reverted to the Crown—"

"Stop," said Noel, glancing up. "He dies later on? In 1724? Leaving no heirs?"

"Affirmative."

"Then it wouldn't matter if he died now," said Noel. "That wouldn't affect history. Say if the storm hits tomorrow and I have to choose between rescuing Lady Pamela or rescuing the boy, then there's no problem. What about Lady Pamela's future? Does she turn up later on?"

"Unknown. Records are incomplete."

"It is the gods who decide if one lives or dies," said Mondoun.

Noel ignored him. "Who else survives?"

"Four slaves, one of whom is a young boy named Kona Masi," replied the LOC. "Later, he is known as Jonah Pontrain. He leads a slave uprising on Barbados—"

"Stop," said Noel. He glanced nervously at Mondoun. He didn't think it was a good idea for the man to hear more.

In the dim glow of light, shadows had crowded around them in the cave. They were especially dark near the *Bocor* as though more than shadows crouched beside him. He sat motionless and slumped, only his eyes moving as he listened. There was something unnatural to his stillness, yet the cave seemed filled with energy and movement on a subconscious level, half-seen, half-felt, a crawling prickle of awareness across Noel's scalp.

Noel stood up, staggered for his balance, and started toward the exit.

Mondoun uncoiled from his slumped position, arching his back. He stretched out his long black arms and hissed like a cobra.

White light flashed in Noel's face, blinding him and driving him backward. He stumbled and had to crouch to keep from falling. His eyes watered and stung, and once he was able to open them again purple splotches marred his vision.

"You have not permission to go," said Mondoun. "If you insult the gods again, even I cannot protect you."

Resentfully Noel turned to face him. "Look, thanks for getting my LOC back for me," he said. "But don't expect—"

"You command a thing of power," said Mondoun as though he had not spoken. "And I command you."

"No way!" said Noel. "You—"

"Silence!" roared Mondoun loudly enough to make the cave shake. "Silence before I make gris-gris of you!"

"Gris-gris," said the LOC's toneless voice. "An amulet or incantation used by people who practice the rites of ancient African religions. Similar to the *grigri* amulet of Bulanda. Cross-indexed to topic heading voodoo, from the Louisiana French word *voudou*, and the African *vo'du'*, its origins are linked to a tutelary deity or—"

"Stop," said Noel, shaken. The LOC was programmed to respond to his voice commands only. It was not supposed to volunteer information. Yet it had just violated both of those parameters. "Run diagnostics—"

"No! No more commands to the demon LOC unless I bid it," said Mondoun. He stood up, seemingly having recovered his strength and energy.

Noel also rose to his feet and faced the taller man. "The LOC is mine. It's not yours to command. It's not yours to use."

Mondoun's dark eyes filled with rage.

Hastily Noel looked away, refusing to be caught in yet another hypnotic spell. "LOC!" he yelled. "Activate electromagnetic damping field and repel all energy forms on your sensory waves."

He didn't know if the LOC could hold off demons or whatever energy forms were swooping around in here. He didn't know if it would protect him from another of Mondoun's spells. But while the LOC pulsed rapidly and an eerie blue light spread through the cave, Noel turned his back on Mondoun and plunged outside, running as fast as his feet would carry him.

CHAPTER 5

He stumbled down the hillside, careening into trees, snagging himself in vines and branches. The blackness of the night turned everything into a menacing unknown. Gusts of wind swayed the bushes, so that he could not tell if the things reaching for him were branches or hands. He slapped and shoved his way through the thicket, aware that he'd lost the trail and not caring. His ears strained behind him for sounds of pursuit, but his own crashing progress and the rumble of thunder overhead drowned other noises out.

Lightning flashed, a jagged bolt of blue-white energy that speared the ground a few meters ahead of Noel. The crackling bang nearly deafened him. Instinctively he threw himself flat, his heart in his mouth, his ears ringing. A tree snapped mortally and caught fire, and the backlash of energy prickled across Noel's skin, vibrating his teeth and making his hair stand on end.

Slowly, appalled at how close it had come, he picked himself up. The air reeked of burned ozone and fire. The orange flames rose skyward, like a beacon.

Noel dragged in a couple of unsteady breaths, trying to calm his whamming heart, and veered away in a new direction.

Lightning flashed again, making him flinch. But this bolt missed the island. He envisioned it striking the churning seas, hissing steam rising in a cloud. Thunder rumbled ominously.

He had lost his sense of direction, but he wasn't worried. The island was small, maybe a mile in length. He couldn't get very lost. In a pinch he could always home in on the beach with the LOC, but right now he was reluctant to activate it in case the *Bocor* was still on his trail.

But Mondoun didn't seem to be following him. Gradually Noel slowed his pace and finally dropped to one knee to catch his breath. It began to rain pounding sheets of water that flattened the vegetation and drenched him in seconds. Noel crawled under a bush with enormous leaves the size of his torso and huddled there.

Irrationally, the pouring rain made him feel safer.

Shoving his dripping hair back from his face, he said, "LOC, activate."

The computer shimmered on, casting a soft light that was diffused by the rain.

"Scan data banks for Baba Mondoun."

The LOC pulsed and hummed for a long time. "No entry found."

"Cross-index search. Reference voodoo. Reference Tortuga. Reference piracy, circa late seventeenth century. Scan."

"Negative entry," said the LOC.

Noel sighed. No matter how many billions of facts were stored in the miniature data banks, the LOC still remained vulnerable to how complete its sources of information were. If there were no birth records, no death certificates, no recorded trial or prison entries, then there was no way to pin down a person. It seemed Baba Mondoun had not made any impact on history.

"LOC, scan data banks for Black Lonigan, pirate captain of the ship *Medusa*, circa late seventeenth century."

"Scanning . . . Lonigan . . . legendary privateer for Charles II of England. Born in Dublin, Ireland, 1612. Started career in Royal Navy as cabin boy, age fourteen, then deserted and joined pirate ship. Later received letter of marque from King Charles, commissioning his ship as a naval vessel during the war with Spain."

"Stop," said Noel in annoyance. "You've got the wrong pirate."

"Data has been entered incorrectly?" asked the LOC.

"I don't know," he replied, shifting himself to avoid water running down his neck. "This man couldn't have been born in 1612. He's not old enough. Scan again."

"Scanning . . . Lonigan, Red . . . born in Dublin, Ireland, 1612."

"Stop. Red Lonigan is the wrong man. I asked about *Black* Lonigan."

"Correction noted. Please give specific instructions."

"I *did*," snapped Noel.

The LOC waited.

Curbing the urge to shake it, Noel said, "Scan for data regarding *Black* Lonigan, late seventeenth century."

"Scanning . . . Lonigan, Black . . . birthdate unknown . . . birthplace Cuba. Father Red Lonigan. Mother Spanish noblewoman kidnapped and held hostage off coast of Florida. Made cabin boy, later elected sailing master. Successful buc-caneer until Treaty of America between Spain and England. During 1690s preyed on coast of North America, chiefly along the Carolinas but with occasional forays into Louisi-ana."

"And now he's come back to the Caribbean," said Noel.

"Affirmative. Lonigan was hanged in August, 1697, follow-ing trial in Port Royal. His crew disbanded. No one found his treasure, supposedly buried on an unnamed island."

"Like this one?" said Noel idly.

"Insufficient data to form a hypothesis."

"So where does this voodoo stuff come in?" wondered Noel aloud.

"Insufficient data to form a hypothesis. Please rephrase question."

"He keeps a tame witch doctor on his ship." Noel blinked and tapped the LOC with his fingertip. "I guess Mondoun really is a witch doctor. Or at least he's gifted with strong telekinetic abilities. He also knows some hypnotic techniques. Where did he learn those?"

"No data available."

"Big help you are."

The LOC pulsed silently.

"Emphasize parameter programming," said Noel sternly. "Emphasize isomorphic control isolation."

"Working."

"You respond only to my voice commands."

"Affirmative."

"You offer data only in response to my direct questions."

"Affirmative."

"Don't forget that," said Noel, wishing he had a better way to scold the computer. All he could do, however, was run diagnostic and emphasis commands. "LOC? I said don't forget that."

"Parameters are functioning."

No, they're not, Noel wanted to say, but he dropped it. He had other questions to ask.

"Scan for anomalies in time stream," he said, yawning. The rain drummed steadily around him, and he was chilled from sitting in the mud. "Has Leon changed history yet?"

"Scanning . . . negative."

"Have I changed history?"

"Qualification. Captain Miller of *Plentitude* died by drowning, not by gunshot, in original time stream. No significant change to history."

"No consequences, you mean."

"Affirmative."

Noel let out his breath. The longer he remained trapped in the past, the greater the odds were that he would really tamper—however inadvertently—with history enough to alter the future. So far, he'd managed to correct his and Leon's interference, but sooner or later one of them was bound to make a big mistake that couldn't be fixed.

At least he was thinking more clearly now than he had been in the voodoo cave. Noel was ashamed that he'd been deliberately plotting ways to have Lady Pamela survive drowning instead of the little boy. Personal feelings could not be allowed to affect the set path of history. His job was not to interfere, not to tamper, not to change anything to suit himself. He was only an observer, a recorder, and an analyst of events. If he ever succumbed to the temptation to determine individual fates according to his own whims, then he would indeed unleash chaos on the future. That was exactly what the anarchists of his own century had wanted him to do when they sabotaged his LOC and trapped him here in the past. He must not lose his perspective. He must not help them succeed in destroying his own time.

"LOC," he said, "since Leon and I haven't changed history this time, how long do we have remaining before recall programming pulls us out?"

"Unknown," said the LOC.

He frowned. "What do you mean, unknown? You have a precise running counter."

"Is that a question?"

"Yes."

"Unknown."

Worried, Noel ran his fingers through his wet hair and thought hard. Travel operated on a forty-nine to one ratio, meaning a normal research mission lasted over two thousand minutes, or about one and a half days in travel time. In real time, he was gone forty-nine minutes, give or take four or five minutes, depending on the dimensional curve and point of entry. Noel had arrived here two and a half days ago. If neither he nor Leon had changed history, then they should have already been yanked out by the standard recall programming.

Until now he hadn't given it much thought, assuming instead that one of them had inadvertently tampered with events. In the two previous travels, their very arrival had changed things and delayed their departure.

"Is safety-chain programming running?" asked Noel.

"Affirmative."

"*Why?*" asked Noel. "I don't understand this. Safety chain is supposed to kick on *only* if we've created a change or anomaly in the time stream. You're saying there isn't one."

"No anomaly."

"Then why is safety chain going? How long are we going to be here? A week? Longer? Are you malfunctioning?"

"Unknown. Unknown. Negative."

Noel snapped the thing off. "Damn!" he said furiously.

Maybe nothing about the LOC was working right now. Its ocean immersion could have completely scrambled its circuits, maybe even shorted its biochip network. Maybe it no longer had the ability to run accurate diagnostic checks and didn't *know* it was malfunctioning.

He was tempted to chuck the thing into the bushes and leave it, but of course his implant wouldn't allow that. And he had no intention of leaving it for Mondoun to find.

"Activate," said Noel. "Prepare to run intensive diagnostics across all—"

"Warning," said the LOC, flashing insistently. "Warning. Message channel open. Message channel open."

It took Noel a moment to understand what that meant. Then he jumped to his feet, heedless of the leaves that dumped water on him or of the rain still pelting down. Hope and relief surged through him. At last, the folks at the Time Institute had figured out he was in trouble and tracked him down. If they could give him instructions, they could help him get home.

"Receive message!" he said eagerly.

The LOC flickered as though its power supply was running low. That was impossible. Its tiny radium power pack had a half-life of two thousand years. Noel shook his wrist and thumped the LOC with his forefinger.

"Receive message!"

Nothing happened. Agonized, Noel shook it again. The last time the Institute had tried to send him a message, Leon's hijinks had caused the message transfer to fail. He couldn't bear to miss them again.

"Scan forward to origin point," he said urgently. "Receive the damned message."

The LOC flickered again, its light so dim it seemed almost extinguished. Then a voice issued forth from it, a deep resonant voice that made icy prickles run along the back of Noel's neck.

"You are mine," the voice intoned. "I have named you so before the dark gods. Come to Baba. *Come.*"

Noel's blood turned to cold slush. His legs felt like someone was stabbing them with ice picks. For an instant he swayed forward as though he would obey the command, then he jerked himself back.

This was no cave full of drugged smoke. He didn't know how the hell Mondoun had tapped into the LOC's message antenna, but he'd had enough of this mumbo-jumbo nonsense.

"Hey, Mondoun!" he said savagely. "Get the hell off this frequency before I kick your butt back to Africa. The only one I belong to is myself. Got it?"

Angrily he tapped the LOC. "Deactivate."

The LOC shut down, and Noel set off through the rain, striding fast, his breath jerking with anger. He'd had it with these weird games. As soon as the storm abated, he was grabbing a dinghy and leaving this island. He could just float out there, with weevily bread and stale water until the recall yanked him to another time and place. And Leon was going with him.

Something about the size of his head flew at him without warning, looming out of the darkness and rain. It struck him in the face. Startled by the touch of wet fur, a fetid stench, and angry squeaks and chitters coming from the animal, Noel yelled and flailed at it instinctively. He drove it off, but it flew back, beating him in the face and chest with its leathery wings, its tiny claws scratching his skin as it fought for purchase.

It was a bat. Revolted, Noel grabbed the thing and flung it away from him. Its needle-sharp teeth sank into the meaty part of his palm, plunging deep. He could sense the thing's greed, could feel it sucking eagerly at his blood. Desperately he swung his arm and crashed the bat into a tree trunk. He managed to dislodge it, and shook his hand—throbbing now—so hard drops of blood splattered.

Uncontrollable shudders ran through him. He turned about in the darkness, looking for it, straining to see through the rain that battered his face. Maybe he'd killed it. God, he hoped so. It was horrible, nasty. He felt unclean, contaminated. He hoped the damned thing wasn't rabid. And the size of it . . . must be a fruit bat or a vampire bat. He shuddered again.

After a few seconds he walked on, shouldering his way through vines and undergrowth. He had just started to relax, to look around him in hopes of finding his bearings, when he stepped knee-deep in water.

Startled, he jumped back, tripped over a root, and floundered a bit until he got back on solid ground. Squinting, he peered ahead at the snarled thicket of trees. He could hear the rain falling on water. The place smelled swampy—dank and stagnant. Some kind of animal screamed in the distance.

Noel jumped, then forced himself to calm down. It was a mangrove swamp, nothing more. All he had to do was skirt it, and he'd be fine. The jungle, after all, was relatively safe. He knew the islands sported little in the way of wildlife other than a few iguanas, some bats, numerous kinds of birds, and an occasional boa constrictor.

Backing up, he turned to his right and started forward. Something hit the back of his neck forcefully, nearly knocking him down. He heard the twittering of a bat, and yelled, twisting and slapping at it to drive it away. Off balance, he staggered around and slammed his shoulder against a tree. He flailed with his hands, slapping the creature that twittered angrily and dived at him again. He couldn't fend this one off no matter how he twisted and struggled. He didn't know if it was the same one or another. All he knew was that it was about the same size as his head, and it stank of dead things. Hysteria burned in him, an irrational panic threatening to burst out of control. He wanted it off, wanted it off *now,* but he knew if he lost his head, then he wouldn't be able to help himself at all.

Then it grabbed the back of his shirt, and its fangs sank into his neck. He felt it suck at him obscenely, felt it drawing his blood, his life.

He yelled again and yanked it off, flinging it forward over his head. Its leathery wings flapped rapidly. Catching a wind current, it swooped and came at him again. Noel plunged into the densest thicket he could find, trying to find refuge. The thing followed him, twittering, its wings rattling against the pounding raindrops. It almost seemed to have an intelligence to it, as though no easier prey would satisfy its hunger, as though it had sought him out in the jungle.

Had Mondoun sent it?

That was crazy. Noel shoved the thought away. He was letting this place get to him, and that was foolish. If he could get away from this damned bat, he'd be fine.

Winded, Noel scrambled faster, scratching his face and hands. He burst from the thicket, dodged the creature that swooped and dived at him, picked up a stick and swung it at the bat.

He connected with a small thud, and the thing shrilled in pain. It went sailing into a bush and did not emerge. Noel slowly lowered the stick. He was breathing hard. Sweat poured off him despite the rain. Gulping for air, he touched the back of his neck, seeking the wound. His fingertip found the two small puncture marks.

"Damn," he said angrily.

More twittering. A rush of leathery wings through the rain. Noel looked up, disbelieving, then ducked as a shape swooped at him, then another, then another. More were coming, their twitters and squeaks angry.

He swung the stick, but there were too many swirling around him now. Panic broke through. Tossing down the stick, he fled as fast as his weary legs could carry him.

For a few seconds he thought he could outrun them, but they streamed after him, wings swishing in the rain, squeaking and diving ahead of him, right into his face as though to cut him off.

Noel skidded to a stop, tried to dodge, and lost his footing in the mud. He slipped and fell. His head thudded against something hard, like a tree root. Blackness rushed at him, but he fought it off, fought to stay conscious, knowing that if he failed they would kill him.

But his head was spinning. He tried to get up, tried to back away from that whirlpool of darkness, tried to make it. But they were on him, crowding and fighting among themselves, hot damp furry bodies jostling each other with furious squeaks. The bites were the last thing he felt.

Bad dreams . . . dreams of fire and drowning . . . dreams of blood.

Choking for air, Leon jerked awake and nearly fell from his hammock. Around him were dozens of snoring men, each suspended in his own hammock. The ship's timbers groaned and creaked softly as the restless, storm-tossed seas shifted her.

He was safe. All was well.

Why then did he feel so breathless, so frightened? He sat up and rubbed his face, trying to pull himself together.

When the storm first hit, the drunken pirates abandoned the beach and took shelter back on the *Medusa*. The big, shallow-hulled ship was battened down, her masts bare, and both anchors mooring her well enough. The bay offered good protection, and even if she was swept out to open sea, she was not likely to come to harm. The sailing master had checked the direction of the wind. They had fifty miles between this island and the next. They could ride out a small storm with that much room.

Something, however, was wrong. His heart speeded up, galloping inside his chest until he gasped for air. Pressing his hand to the right side of his chest, Leon dragged in a series of deep breaths in an effort to calm himself.

He frowned, not wanting to face the fact, yet knowing he had to. Something was wrong with Noel.

Something had been wrong all day, ever since Noel and Baba Mondoun came face-to-face. Leon could not read Mondoun's mind, and he didn't want to. There were void pockets in Mondoun's mind, places and sections where nothing existed, just dark blankness amid the shapes and patterns of his thoughts. Leon did not think he wanted to venture too close to someone with a mind like that.

When Mondoun had looked at Noel on the deck today, Noel had gone blank. He vanished, psychically. Of course he would not listen to Leon, but Leon had tried his best to warn the fool to take care.

Now Leon left his hammock and went quietly up on deck. Around him the storm raged on, buffeting his clothes as though it would tear them off his back, lashing him with rain that stung like needles, shrieking and hammering at the ship as though it meant to tear her apart.

Standing at the railing, Leon faced the dim blur of the island in the darkness and reached out with his mind for Noel.

Nothing.

He shivered, frightened by that loss of contact. Although he could not read or manipulate Noel's mind the way he could many others, he was always linked to his twin. Now that link was gone. Leon hugged himself and put his back to the wind.

Freedom?

Or loneliness?

He still felt uneasy, restless. His mouth was dry, so dry he found it difficult to swallow. He was sweating beneath his oilskins. His heart still went too fast.

Noel?

The connection returned with an unexpected force that was like a blow. Staggered, Leon gasped aloud and bent over, trying to hang on to his own identity as a maelstrom of alien emotions and thoughts barreled through him.

Noel afraid. Noel running for his life through the jungle. Noel trapped out there, stalked by something he could not comprehend. Noel fighting things fashioned from that awful nothingness. Noel losing, overwhelmed, going down. . . .

"*No!*" cried Leon in anguish.

Shuddering, he managed just in time to snap the contact, to withdraw before the harm traveled across into *him*. But it had sensed him in that split second. Sensed and turned toward him.

Leon paced the rail, staggering now and then to keep his balance as the ship yawed on her moorings. She dragged anchor a bit, shuddering through her length. Near the stern, the sailing master and another figure Leon didn't recognize were conferring with rapid gestures and shouts lost in the wind.

Noel was a fool, always a fool. He never tried to make any gain for himself, refused to accept the fact that they would never go back to the twenty-sixth century, and seemed determined to make things harder on himself than necessary. Furthermore, he wouldn't listen to Leon, wouldn't accept Leon, wouldn't make any truce. He thought he had the right to dictate what Leon should and shouldn't do. He thought being the original made him superior.

He was wrong. He was stupid.

He was also in trouble.

Leon frowned, worried more than he wanted to admit. There was something horrible out there on that island. Leon believed in protecting his own hide first.

But when things hurt Noel, they hurt Leon too. He could feel pain in his hand, pain in his laboring lungs, pain elsewhere. It wasn't his. He bitterly resented the fact that he was doomed to forever experience Noel's sensations while denied his own.

Yet he dared not abandon Noel now. He did not think he could exist if Noel ceased to. And Leon was very, very afraid of dying.

With a growl, he climbed over the side, struggling down the boarding net to the dinghy. Unshipping the oarlocks, he pulled away, and nearly capsized in the rough waves before he found the rhythm of rowing and could really put his back and shoulders into it.

He misjudged the breakers, which flipped the dinghy sideways and drove it through the lacy surf onto the beach. Jumping out, he heaved the dinghy up far enough where the tide wouldn't drag it out to sea.

Puffing hard from his exertions, he looked around through the rain and the shadows at the sodden ashes and trampled sand of their evening camp. He listened inside, hoping he didn't open himself to the dark thing out there.

At last, he touched a glimmer of Noel. He started forward, knowing the direction he needed to take, but the sight of a figure coming across the beach stopped him.

Despite the darkness, the height and forceful, long-limbed stride told Leon it was Black Lonigan. He was carrying something across his shoulder.

Noel.

Leon held his breath and watched, feeling as though his feet were frozen to the sand. His twin wasn't dead. For now that was enough.

Black Lonigan didn't seem surprised to see him. He stopped just short of Leon. "Good," he said in his gravelly voice. "Ye brought the dinghy at the right time. Well done, Leon."

Puzzled, for Lonigan had given him no orders to come here, Leon opened his mouth, then at the last moment changed what he'd been about to say. "That's Noel," he said.

"Yes."

"Is—is he drunk?"

Lonigan stepped past him and headed for the dinghy, obliging Leon to follow him. Not until he slung Noel's unconscious form into the dinghy did he glance at Leon.

"Ye know the true answer," he said. "Don't pretend."

Leon felt as though he were made of crystal, and this man could see everything. It was supposed to be the other way around. "What's wrong with him? I came because he needed help."

"Be ye linked, then? Good. Twins are favored by the *loas*."

"The what?"

Lonigan only laughed and gave the dinghy a shove. "Ye'll learn."

Leon leaned over and touched Noel's face. It was very cold and still beneath the rain. "What's wrong with him?"

"He is being prepared," said Lonigan.

The pirate shoved the dinghy into waist-deep water and climbed in. Leon had to scramble quickly to join him. Once there, sitting across from the pirate with Noel's body, Leon wasn't so sure he'd been wise to get in. Lonigan seemed spiky at the edges. His aura held blood.

"Prepared for what?"

Lonigan laughed. "To be Mondoun's servant. There be much spirit in him, this twin of yours. Much temper and much independence. That will change once the *loa* possesses him. Oh, Baron Samedi is very pleased to have this body marked for his use."

Alarm rose in Leon. He didn't like where this was heading. "Who is Baron Samedi?"

"Lord of the dead. Very powerful. Very dark. With this *loa* in Noel, Baba Mondoun will be unrivaled among all the *Bocors*

and the *mambas*. He will drive away the *Houngons* and unleash
great power over the seas. Then I shall rule all the pirates, and
their treasure will belong to me."

Leon swallowed and kept silent. He didn't know what to
say. Now, however, he knew why Noel had been afraid.

I warned you, Noel, he thought resentfully. *I did my best to
warn you, but you wouldn't listen.*

With rising worry, he thought about what might happen to
him if Noel was possessed. He didn't want to be sucked back
into the time vortex again.

"Heave to, lad!" said Lonigan while Leon struggled with the
oars. "Yer a lubber with this dinghy. Head for the *Plentitude.*"

Leon stared through the rain at the merchant ship. She was
dragging her anchors a bit, and was close enough to the mouth
of the small bay to be in danger of having the tide carry
her out.

"The *Medusa* is safer in this storm," said Leon, gasping
when the waves tossed them high. "Harley says the glass is
still falling. He's afraid it may be a hurricane."

"Naw, too early in the year," said Lonigan scornfully.

"Harley said hurricanes can happen in June."

"Harley's an old woman when it comes to a spot of rough
weather. It's the *Rada.*"

"The what?"

"The white gods. They fear what's coming. They want to
make trouble for us."

With the wind shrieking in his ears and trying to rip the hair
from his head, with the whitecaps tossing the dinghy like a
toy and sloshing over the sides so that Lonigan had to start
bailing, Leon thought Lonigan was being far too casual about
the storm.

"The *Medusa* is safer," he said again. "Her flat bottom makes
her more stable and—"

"Lad, don't be telling me about my own ship!"

"The *Plentitude* is older, and she has a leak below the
waterline. Even with men on the pumps, she isn't—"

"Avast!" shouted Lonigan. "Mondoun wants a sacrifice. He
wants a young heart, and a place of death."

Startled, Leon stopped rowing. "Death! What do you mean?"

"She'll sink tomorrow," said Lonigan. "It has been foretold. Baron Samedi must come into a place of death."

"But—"

"Keep arguing with me, ye damned puppy, and I'll heave ye overboard!" roared Lonigan. "We're doing as Baba says, do ye follow? Interfere in this, and he'll put a *loa* into ye as well."

Lonigan believed all right, and he would carry out his threats if Leon didn't back off. Leon looked down at Noel, still unconscious, and felt the old jealousy twist hard.

"We are linked," he said. "If Noel is possessed by the spirit, what will happen to me?"

Lonigan's laughter boomed out. "Baba will make a potion to protect ye. Don't quake yer boots. Ye still be valuable to me."

CHAPTER 6

With the dinghy secured to the anchor chain, Lonigan called out his orders to the watchman. Soon a boatswain's chair was lowered to them. Noel's unconscious body was secured in it, and he was hoisted up to the deck while Leon and Lonigan climbed the boarding net hanging over the side.

In the wild wet, with waves crashing over them and the ropes slippery from water, Leon choked, sputtered, and struggled to make it, fearing at any moment he would be swept away and drowned. Lonigan passed him easily, then leaned over the railing to drag him the rest of the way.

Belly down on the deck, Leon gasped for air and wondered why he'd ever left the comfortable safety of his hammock on the *Medusa.*

Despite the late hour, it seemed no one slept aboard the *Plentitude.* The skeleton crew came running. "Captain! Captain!" cried one, throwing himself at Lonigan's feet. "The gods have turned their faces from us. Call back their favor."

"Quartermaster," said another, less frightened voice. "We need to put her out to sea. We'll be run aground soon."

Belatedly Leon realized the man was addressing him. Leon hesitated, at a loss to know what order to give. When they had been dividing the booty, he'd enjoyed his new position of high status. Now he could only stare in indecision, humiliation burning in his face.

"I said we need to weigh anchor," said the man, more insistently. "We'll run aground—"

"And if you leave harbor the winds will blow you into the next island before you can raise sail," said Lonigan harshly. His voice had become curt and harsh; he sounded like the leader Leon had first met. Leon had joined him because he'd felt drawn to the charisma of this man. Now he felt it again.

Lonigan gestured angrily. "Are ye daft? There's no sea room in the Antilles. This isn't the Atlantic, where ye can let a storm sweep ye two hundred miles off course."

"The Navy always—"

"The Navy be damned!" said Lonigan. The other pirates murmured agreement with him. "Navy ways are not the ways of the Brotherhood. We know these islands. Until ye do, keep quiet."

"But, Captain," said the man, "the wind's circular."

Lonigan paused. "Eh?"

"Aye. I've checked. Remember the long swell and the way the clouds looked today? I think it's a hurricane."

"We've got to get out, then," said Lonigan. "Can ye navigate a semicircle?"

"Aye, I think—"

Lonigan clapped him on the shoulder. "Get aboard the *Medusa*! Prepare to weigh anchor. I'll join ye in a moment."

The men scattered. Lonigan turned on Leon and gripped his arm hard. "Get below, quickly, and find me a child and a woman."

Leon stared at him. "You mean the passengers? Lady—"

"Fool! Check among the slaves first. Do it quickly. We haven't much time."

"Is your black magic more important than getting out of here?"

Lonigan struck him in the face. Leon staggered back, putting his hand to his jaw. Inside he felt rage boil hot. On the deck, Noel moaned and stirred. Lonigan stamped his foot upon Noel's back, pinning him down.

"Go, I say! Do as yer told, ye ignorant piece of shark bait, or I'll—"

"I joined you as an equal," said Leon resentfully. "I've offered to share all my knowledge with you. Don't treat me like a—"

Lonigan's fist hammered him into the railing. Clutching his stomach and wheezing for breath, Leon lost track of what he'd been about to say.

Lonigan gripped his arm again. "Now listen, ye fool. I know who has the power and who has the knowledge. It's your brother."

"Wrong!" shouted Leon furiously. "Once, maybe, but not anymore! I took his power from him. I—"

Lonigan reached down and lifted Noel's left arm. Yanking back Noel's sleeve, he revealed the LOC fastened on Noel's wrist, undisguised, undeniably real.

Leon stared, his mouth open, his mind blank with astonishment. "But I destroyed it," he whispered. "I got rid of it. I made him give it to me, and I got rid of it."

Lonigan dropped Noel's arm. It thudded on the deck, slack and lifeless. "Baba brought the thing of power back," he said. "Now will ye serve me, or will ye end our association? Know this. The only thing the dark gods savor more than the heart of an innocent child is the quivering entrails of a coward . . . served *hot*."

Leon backed up a step, his mouth dry, his heart thudding. "What—what about the storm?" he stammered.

"Go," said Lonigan.

Stumbling over his own feet, Leon hurried to do his bidding.

The hold was a stinking, black maw filled with the groaning of stressed timbers, the wails of frightened slaves, the squeaking of rats, and the rumbling shift of crates and barrels insufficiently secured.

Holding a lantern high, Leon picked his way through the mass of suffering humanity. The stench was as thick as a wall. Dark faces, marked by tribal tattoos and scars, stared back at him. Eyes worn blank with pain, hunger, and sickness shimmered in the light. Some of them were dead, and should have already been thrown overboard. The corpses lay chained to terrified companions. Some still possessed enough spirit to lunge at him like wild dogs, snapping with their teeth. Cursing,

Leon beat them back with a belaying pin.

Normally he would have been drunk on their fear. The emotions of others were like meat and drink to him. To be their master, to have the right to beat them as he pleased, to say who was to participate in Lonigan's mumbo-jumbo and who was to be spared should have been an exquisite pleasure. But Leon was too worried to enjoy himself right now.

He had intended to form a partnership with Lonigan. The man was ruthless, successful, and rich. Glimpses into his mind had shown Leon that he had a fabulous trove of treasure hidden away somewhere on this tiny island. Leon thought he could sway the man, and when he was elected quartermaster within a few hours of joining the crew it seemed to be working. Yet the weird voodoo beliefs of Lonigan were an unexpected problem. Besides, Lonigan had too much interest in Noel. Now that Noel had his LOC back, damn him, he was again the valuable one. Leon felt he had become expendable in Lonigan's eyes. Already Lonigan was treating him like a servant. It was only a matter of time before he became even less.

Toward this end of the hold, water was sloshing over the boards. About a third of the slaves were lying in it. Leon wondered if anyone was manning the pumps right now. He also thought about the information that the *Plentitude* was supposed to sink tomorrow. Fresh sweat broke out across him. He considered sneaking off the ship and taking refuge on the island, but he couldn't go there alone. He couldn't exist alone. Without the energy of other people to live on, he grew too weak to resist the pull of the time vortex.

He needed a plan, an idea of how to escape Lonigan. More than that, he wanted to steal Lonigan's treasure. Somehow he needed to peer into Lonigan's mind more deeply than he had heretofore dared. Lonigan would have to be distracted. Perhaps during the voodoo ceremony Leon would get a chance.

A fresh sense of urgency gripped him. The sooner the ceremony started, the sooner he could get out of here.

He found a woman, bare-breasted and clothed only in a loincloth and a necklet of beads. Her nose was pierced and she had three parallel scars on each cheek. She held a toddler, rocked it steadily in her arms while she crooned an eerie, monotonous sound.

Leon shone the lantern over them. The child was dead, had been dead for some time. Its glassy eyes, crusted lips, and small bloated body reached something inside Leon. He looked away quickly, swallowing hard, and closed his eyes to link himself with the woman. Her grief pierced him like the stab of a spear. He was unprepared for the raw intensity of it and staggered back, breaking the link in desperation.

Gasping, he wiped sweat from his brow and glanced down to see the woman staring up at him. She stopped crooning, but her body went on rocking the child as though it could do nothing else. Her eyes were a light, clear brown. They held a flood of anguish and hatred like a barrier against the probing of his mind.

Mutely she held up her child to him. Leon shook his head. For the first time in his short existence he was conscious of having intruded, of having violated a place of privacy where he had no right to enter.

He wanted only to get out of here, to find someone else to serve Lonigan's and Mondoun's purpose.

The woman, however, crawled after him as far as her shackles would permit. She clanked her chains and spoke to him in a hoarse, cracked voice, using a language he did not comprehend.

Noel had the translator, of course. Noel had everything.

But Leon had telepathy, and although he tried to shut off the link he had inadvertently established with the woman, still her thoughts came to him, broken and incomprehensible at first, then clearer, supporting the African dialect she spoke.

" . . . pale god . . . power . . . make Hana live . . . please make my son Hana to live again. Thou has the power to return the light to his small body. Have mercy, O great pale one. Have mercy upon this woman and her son."

Around her other slaves had sat up; some listened and others watched. Leon could feel their intensity. Anger, fear, savage thoughts of revenge, and supplication mingled in his mind. He sipped it, trying to distract himself, trying to escape the woman's mind, which beat at his with a desperation he could not evade.

"Please, baba. Please have mercy on Hana. The elder witches prophesied he would make himself a great warrior one day. He would lead nations. He would have many riches and many wives. Thou are great, pale god. Thou has the power to restore light to his eyes. Make him laugh again, baba. Oh, holy one, have mercy upon this woman and her son."

Kneeling, she held out the child in supplication. Leon backed away still farther. The pathetic stillness of that small face tore at him. He wanted to gag. He wanted to yell at the woman to leave him alone. He wanted to run, yet he remained rooted there among them, held by the force of their desperation and suffering, overwhelmed by the injustice of their plight.

Living only to feed upon the thoughts and passions of others, lacking any of his own save his undying resentment of his brother, Leon found himself trapped by them.

A man raised a chant, an eerie, ululating cry that made Leon's heart contract. Their minds beat at him like bats swooping from a cave. He instinctively raised his arms, yet when he realized that he was physically cringing from these chained prisoners, he stiffened his body and tried to force his feet to carry him out of there.

"What the bloody hell is all this racket?" shouted a voice from the ladder leading out from the hold. "Leon, be ye still down here then?"

Leon tried to answer; his voice lacked enough air.

"Leon!"

He swallowed and succeeded in making sound. "Yes?"

"What be takin' ye all day? Lonigan's raisin' hell on deck. Unchain one of the damned darkies and bring 'im up."

Leon looked down and saw the ring of skeleton keys dangling from his nerveless fingers. He forced his mind to work. "There are dead ones down here. They need to be cleaned out."

"What? Oh, hell."

Clumping footsteps came down the ladder. One of the pirates, a short, bandy-legged man named Walter Griffin entered the amber lantern light. He stood there with his feet braced wide apart, balancing against the heave and toss of the groaning ship, and glared about him.

"Gad, they're chained down too tight amongst each other. No wonder part of 'em is dead. There'll be disease next. The filthy greedy blighters what run these merchant ships, crammin' too much in, and no ballast trim to make a proper run, hell! Small wonder they be easy pickin's fer us, eh? Which is it, then? Lonigan's witch doctor's got to make one of his dances for the darkies in the crew." The man rolled his eyes and winked. "You know how they get on a raw night like this. Get to wantin' their religion, eh?" He laughed. "And Lonigan's more superstitious than any of them."

Leon managed only a sickly grin. Griffin's presence had broken the spell. He glanced around and found himself trapped by the mother's pleading gaze again.

He gestured at her. "She can't hold that child. She—"

"Aye, we'll take her up," said Griffin. Plucking the keys from Leon's hand, he unlocked the woman's shackles. "Come on, lass. Time to give your poor heathen babe a decent burial."

Leon glanced around for the second victim. He swung the lantern in a high arc, sending the light across the slaves' dark bodies. They writhed away from the light, murmuring in their own tongues. An image of black mambo snakes, wriggling furiously and deadly with venom, entered Leon's mind. He shivered and thrust the image away.

Only one individual did not cringe from the light. He was a half-grown boy, scrawny, with awkward arms and legs too long for the rest of him. His features were thin-lipped and chiseled. Although he was as filthy and as skinned-up as the rest of them, he still carried himself with pride. His wide eyes gazed steadily at Leon with far too much intelligence.

One corner of his mouth curved up slightly as though he had seen how his companions held Leon captive for a few moments. Leon's resentment flared. He pointed at the boy. "That one, too."

Griffin was busy wrapping the dead child in a scrap of sail-cloth. He tossed Leon the keys, and seething at his impudence

Leon unshackled the boy himself.

"Get up," said Leon, *pushing* with his mind to reinforce the order. He saw the boy flinch slightly, and some of his anger cooled off. Satisfied, he prodded the boy to his feet and gestured for him to climb the ladder.

Topside, the wind gusted so fiercely Leon feared he would be blown off deck and into the raging water. He caught a glimpse of the *Medusa*, close reefed, heading out to sea. He gripped the railing in panic. Lonigan had abandoned him, had left him aboard a ship destined to sink. It wasn't fair.

One of the black pirates seized the slaves and hustled them toward the poop. Another plucked at Leon's arm. "Hurry, hurry!" he said. "Until the gods are happy again, this storm will blow us all to pieces."

The once Spàrtan but comfortable captain's quarters of the *Plentitude* had been reduced to a shambles. Walking in, Leon blinked at the dazzling amount of light coming from dozens of thick tallow candles burning from every available corner. The furniture had been shoved aside, and as many of the skeleton crew as could be spared from manning the ship and could fit inside were crammed along the walls and perched on the narrow bunk. With the exception of a few sunburned or freckled faces, most of them were black. Their faces were shiny with sweat. They reminded Leon of ravens perched over carrion. Lonigan, the coward, was not present. Leon's fury grew.

In the center of the room, Noel lay on a plank stretched between two chairs. The pitch of the ship made it likely that his unconscious form would tumble off at any moment. Around them the ship groaned, and the wind was a howling beast clawing to get inside. Leon could smell the fear, could almost put out his tongue and taste the fear.

But there was more than fear inside this stuffy, crowded room. There was a current of anticipation as hot as fire, crackling like the lightning outside.

The two slaves were shoved forward, bringing with them the stench of the hold. They crouched on the floor, the woman moaning to herself, the boy wide-eyed.

A fire built in a brazier over a bucket of sand flared brightly. Several pirates cried out in island patois. One man began to beat a drum.

The door opened, bringing the lash of rain inside and a welcome gust of coolness. Several candles blew out, then the door slammed shut and Lady Pamela and the small boy Neddie Sinclair stood dripping before them. The little boy was rubbing sleep from his eyes and whimpering. Lady Pamela, her brown hair soaked and wind-whipped to a tangle, pressed him against her wide skirts. Her green eyes blazed defiance at everyone, and Leon found himself staring at her.

When she finally stopped looking around at the crowd of pirates and let her gaze fall on Noel, she gasped aloud and pressed her hand to her mouth. Much of the defiance sagged from her shoulders, and she grew ordinary and bedraggled.

She started toward Noel, but stopped. Leon pushed her aside and bent over his twin. In the flickering candlelight, Noel's face looked bruised and scratched. One of his eyes was swollen with a red welt across it. His clothes were torn and filthy with mud and leaf bits. There were numerous small puncture wounds on his neck and arms as though he'd been repeatedly bitten by some tiny animal. His face was as pale as cotton. Despite the oppressive heat, he wasn't sweating.

Frowning, Leon touched him and found Noel's skin cold. Yet he wasn't dead. Leon reached out with his mind across the link and *pushed*.

Nothing.

Noel's mind remained impervious to his control. He'd never been able to manipulate his twin that way. But he needed Noel to regain consciousness and help him if his plan was to work.

He touched Noel's shoulder hesitantly, then gave him a hard shake. "Noel!" he whispered.

"Get back from him!" yelled a furious pirate.

"Don't touch him!"

"He is sacred!"

The yells came from all sides. Leon hesitated, wary of their furious eyes, and lost his chance. Two burly pirates seized him and dragged him away from Noel. He struggled, but one knotted a short length of rope into a noose and tether and slipped it over Leon's head.

He glared at Leon and gave the rope a slight tug. At once Leon felt the noose pull tight against his throat. His breathing shortened, and he glared back at the pirate, seeking to command the man's mind. Nothing. His thoughts bounced off the pirate as though the man was sheathed in glass.

"You interfere again in the captain's doings, and I'll snap your neck," said the pirate.

He tugged again, and the rope burned Leon's skin. He got the message. Furious at his helplessness, he stood there, wishing he'd never given way to that momentary lapse of jealousy and helped Lonigan bring Noel here. Instead, he and Noel had to get away, destroy the LOC once and for all, and find Lonigan's treasure. Then they could stay in this place and time. They could build a life for themselves. They would have enough wealth to do whatever they pleased. They were smarter than the barbaric buffoons of this backward century. They were bound to succeed.

But first Noel had to wake up.

He *pushed* at his twin with his mind. *Noel! Wake up, damn you!*

Noel's eyelids flickered. He stirred slightly.

Encouraged, Leon tried again. *Noel, listen to me. Wake up. Mondoun is going to make a zombie out of you if you don't wake up.*

Noel moaned. He was coming around. Leon reached out in one last *push,* but just then a trapdoor in the floor burst open, and a skeleton levitated into the room from below.

Several men cried out in fear. Leon stood rooted, trying to disbelieve the apparition, trying to probe into the mind controlling this image, trying to dispel it.

He failed.

The skeleton rose higher and higher into the air, until the naked skull bobbed mere inches below the ceiling beams. The bones were bleached clean, gleaming white in the candle-light. They even rattled—a dry, disturbing sound—as the thing bobbed and swayed. The skull wavered on the stacked neck vertebrae, making the lower jaw chatter. Smoke curled out through the empty eye sockets and began to swirl through the air in intricate patterns.

"Mother of God, what is this thing?" said Lady Pamela. She gripped Neddie close, turning his head away so that he might not see what was happening.

Excitement gripped the room, overriding the fear. The pirates were leaning forward, eyes gleaming and teeth bared. The drum beats quickened, pulsing and pounding, throbbing like the rush of blood through Leon's veins.

"Yabo, baba. Yabo, baba."

The chant started soft and grew in volume. Leon felt the hypnotic pull of it. The words flowed through him like warm liquid. Glancing around, he saw everyone except Lady Pamela chanting; even the frightened slaves on the floor added their voices. The urge to join in swelled Leon's throat, but he held back. He manipulated others when he could. He didn't let them manipulate him.

Lady Pamela's face was so white she looked as though she might swoon. Her eyes darted with fear. Leon caught her gaze with his own and probed her mind lightly. He discovered a maelstrom of disgust, horror, fear for the child, fascination, a touch of contempt, and raging curiosity for why she and the little boy were present. Turning his head, Leon swept his mind cautiously about the room and tuned in to the drummer. This man's skin was a light dusky color, revealing his mulatto origins. Whippet-thin, he sat with his legs coiled around his drum and swayed eagerly to the tempo his hands beat out. His mind lusted for Baba Mondoun's appearance. He could barely contain his impatience to see the dark gods summoned. He craved the excitement of watching *loas* possess a body, of seeing it dance and writhe. Even more, he hoped the good *loas* would come too, possessing the body of another in an effort to quell the power of the *Congo*. The danger of sacrificing a child to the dark gods could be seen by the lashing fury of the storm around them, but the drummer only threw back his head with maniacal laughter, enjoying the thrill of braving the *Rada*'s anger.

Leon withdrew his mind and *pushed* at Noel.

No response. He had lost whatever tiny contact he'd had with Noel's subconscious.

Frustrated, increasingly alarmed, Leon glanced at Lady Pamela.

She was staring at the skeleton, now almost obscured by the smoke trails swirling into an elaborate *vèvè* in midair. Men moaned, and the sound sent shivers up Leon's spine. They were running out of time. The smoke *vèvè* was almost complete, and he suspected that when it was finished, Mondoun was going to appear and make real trouble.

Leon *pushed* Lady Pamela's mind with his. She was resistant, but her rising fear made her susceptible, and he captured control.

Knock Noel off the board, he commanded. *Now.*

She hesitated, her face slack, the fierceness now blanked from her green eyes. She took one small step toward Noel, then paused. Her head turned back to gaze at the suspended skeleton.

The smoke was curling down near the floor. The pattern was complete. Leon felt a burst of completely irrational fear.

Now, he screamed at her.

Pushing Neddie aside, she walked toward Noel, but before she reached him, there came a tremendous bang and crash as though lightning had struck the ship. White light flared in the room, dazzling Leon's eyes and causing many to yell, then all the candles went out, plunging them into darkness. The oxygen in the air seemed to vanish, and for a moment Leon felt as though he was being sucked back into the awful vacuum of the time vortex.

He was dissolving, losing cohesion. He screamed and fought to hold himself within reality.

Then air rushed back into the room. With it came light, but not the amber candlelight of before. No, now the room was lit by a strange orange glow spilling up from the open trapdoor.

It was a kind of light that belonged neither to this century nor to this world. Leon stared at it, fighting to cling to his twenty-sixth-century beliefs and sophistication, but goose bumps rose all over him.

The smoke *vèvè* was dissipating slowly, the intricate curls spreading through the room as though to contaminate the air with the spell. As the smoke thinned, and the lambent light glowed more brightly, Leon squinted at the skeleton levitating in the air and realized that it was no longer a skeleton but a man, a black man with bones painted crudely on his chest, arms, and legs in white. Leon blinked. It was Mondoun, wearing nothing but a loincloth, a frizzy, powdered wig, and an absurd tricorne hat. His face was painted skull white also, with dark sockets left around his eyes.

Those eyes snapped open, and there were screams.

"Baba!" cried several voices.

The drumbeats started again, and Baba Mondoun raised one long arm and threw a handful of a powdered substance through the trapdoor into the source of the orange light. Smoke belched forth, stinking of sulfur and something Leon could not identify. In his other hand, Mondoun held the carcass of a macaw, headless, its bright blue and gold plumage bedraggled. He cried out a word that made his worshippers moan, and swung the dead bird through the air.

Droplets of blood splattered the room. Some landed on Noel, still unconscious. Some landed on Leon, burning his skin. He cried out and slapped at himself. The heat in the room intensified suddenly, and the slave woman screamed.

Jumping to her feet, she began to dance wildly to the throbbing tempo of the drumbeats. Holding her arms high in the air, she gyrated around Mondoun as he walked slowly forward to the center of the room. He towered over Noel's helpless form. Drawing a handful of flour from a leather pouch, he drew a *vèvè* upon Noel's bare chest.

Some of the other pirates joined in the dance with the slave woman, leaping like crazy men and howling with an insanity that made Leon's head ring.

He felt the temptation to dance rising through his body. He felt the heat coiling inside his limbs. The drumming vibrated his chest; his heart kept rhythm with it. Ordinarily he would have joined them in any evil they wanted to do without a qualm. He thrived on the darkness within others; he sipped it like nectar.

But this was different. This darkness overtaking the room tonight was not mankind's wickedness or the base weaknesses of greed, lust, and cowardice. It came from something alien, something not human, something ancient and rotted, like damnation personified.

Leon could not accept it. He didn't know whether he had too much of Noel in him, or whether it was his own pride in his abilities, but he could feel it pressed against his mind, seeking entry, a thing oily and cold, its touch so repugnant he shuddered. He would *not* be manipulated. He would *not* be controlled.

With a gasp, he repelled the *loa*. For an instant he saw a dim outline of an ethereal shape dart from him to Lady Pamela, recoil, and slam into a bearded, one-legged pirate. Howling, the man began whirling on his good leg like a dervish, holding his wooden leg out like a scythe.

Mondoun was singing, using old words, power words, words Leon did not want to comprehend from fear that he might succumb to them.

"Noel, damn you! Wake up!" he yelled.

Mondoun's eyes sought Leon's. He curled back his lips to bare his filed teeth. They looked black in this light. Smoke curled slightly from his mouth.

"He cannot hear you. My little ones did their work well." Mondoun held up a small stoppered vial. "They brought me his blood."

Leon's mouth went bone-dry.

Mondoun hissed and held up another vial. "This is the blood of rats taken from the hold. This is the blood of a chicken. This is poison milked from the venom sacks of a toad. These are the special herbs, grown on Hispaniola, dried and ground to fine powder. This is the bowl for the boy's heart. I shall burn it over the fire." He pointed at the dead coals on the brazier, and fire burst to sudden life.

Leon wanted to beg him to choose someone else, but he knew it was futile. Fear coiled deep down inside him, and the old rage came back. If only he could be free of his link to Noel, if only he didn't have to fear that Noel's death would make him die too, *then* he could know freedom. He wouldn't care a jot for what became of his twin. But he could not escape. And he could not enjoy Noel's helplessness now or the danger he was in. No, Leon was forced to risk his neck to protect the one creature he hated most of all. It was not right.

"You resisted the *loa* that sought you out," said Mondoun. "You resisted the honor of serving the *Congo* and the *Pétro*. You have proven yourself unworthy of trust."

Leon dragged his attention back to Mondoun. "If you kill him, I will die too. If you hurt him, I will know his pain. If you rob him of his soul and his mind, I will have nothing."

Even as he spoke, he knew his plea was futile. Mondoun wasn't listening to anything but the madness in his own heart.

Mondoun leaned across Noel's body and peered deep into Leon's eyes. "Your cleverness blinds you. Prove yourself as my servant. Serve the dark gods, and I promise you will not lose the bonds you share with this one."

It had to be a trap. Leon hesitated, his mind frantically turning over his options. "What must I do?" he asked reluctantly.

Mondoun hissed, his eyes wild, their pupils reflecting the dancing flames in the brazier. Smoke curled from his nostrils and lips. He handed Leon a dagger, its honed blade gleaming in the strange light.

"Cut out the child's heart."

Leon's fingers seemed nerveless. He closed them around the hilt of the dagger, yet the knife seemed to weigh a ton. It was all he could do not to drop it. A memory flash came to him of the relentless heat and sunshine of New Mexico, of the young boy Cody dying in Noel's arms. Noel had blamed him for that death, and Noel's fury had been hurled at him like a hammer blow. It had hurt, that anger coming across the link to stab again and again. Leon had never believed that Noel could hurt him, would want to hurt him. But Noel had loved the boy like a younger brother, and there was grief behind his anger. Noel had never loved Leon, had never accepted him as a brother, would never accept him.

What would Noel think of him if he now did as Mondoun demanded?

What would he think of himself?

I am supposed to be wicked, Leon thought bitterly. *I was created without conscience. Noel has it all. Why should I try to change? Why should I even care?*

He lifted the dagger and turned around to look first at the slave boy hunkered on the floor, all bones and tatters, the whip scars crisscrossed on his back. Then he looked at Neddie with his shining curls and pale, pampered skin, hiding in the woman's skirts like a juicy little morsel.

Despising himself, Leon said, "Which one, Baba?"

CHAPTER 7

Lying trapped in the strange limbo that had held him since Mondoun's bats attacked him in the jungle, Noel heard the surrender in Leon's voice. Until now, he had been hopeful that Leon would finally show some decent qualities, but Leon's willingness to kill a child indicated that he was even more degraded and horrible than Noel had ever suspected.

Furious with him, Noel did his best to break free of the queer paralysis that bound his limbs. He could not open his eyes, or move, or speak. Inside, he screamed at Leon not to do it, but the mental link that Leon said connected them did not work both ways. Noel had never been able to reach his duplicate. He could not do it now, no matter how much he strained.

However, he had to do something. He refused to lie here helpless and let this barbarism continue.

His eyes darted behind his closed eyelids, which felt as though they had been glued shut. His straining ears picked up myriad sounds: hoarse breathing, the thud of bare feet dancing on the plank floor, the groans and cries uttered mindlessly in time with the drumbeats. He could smell Mondoun standing beside him, reeking of tannis root, comfrey, sulfur. The flour of the *vèvè* pattern sifted down like delicate dust upon his chest, and once again he was helpless to shake it off.

He knew he was lying on a board, suspended above the floor. The room was suffocatingly hot, yet he wasn't sweating. Beside him, Mondoun was chanting his mumbo-jumbo and mixing his vile ingredients into a bowl.

Noel listened to each liquid splash into the bowl next to him and wondered, *Is that my blood he's pouring in now, or the bird's?* There was no way he would swallow such nauseating stuff.

Somehow he had to break free of his paralysis and roll off the board. That would disrupt the ceremony and maybe bring Leon back to his senses.

But Noel knew he couldn't count much on his duplicate helping. Leon was too susceptible to evil. Given a choice, he always went the wrong way, as he had done now.

Gathering all his will, Noel strained to move his leg, just one leg, hoping that if he could shift it off the board he might succeed in overbalancing his weight.

He strained until red swam across the darkness behind his eyelids. He strained until he could not breathe. He strained until he felt the pain of muscle cramps, but he managed nothing more than a slight twitch of his foot.

"Quickly!" commanded Mondoun from beside him. "Leon, take the heart from the white child and throw it on the fire."

Noel tensed. *No, Leon!*

He heard a woman scream and the sounds of a scuffle. Then Lady Pamela's voice rang out, "By God's good mercy, you will not do it!"

Then her hand gripped Noel's shoulder. She yanked, dragging him off the plank. He hit the floor with a jolt that knocked half the breath from his lungs, and hit his head in the process. His eyes flew open, and in that split second he realized the spell was broken.

He tried to jump to his feet, and found he couldn't quite command his limbs. His legs were like rubber. His arms had no strength. Above him, Mondoun was roaring obscenities. Two men had gripped Lady Pamela's arms, holding her prisoner, and Mondoun brandished his knife at her.

Noel rolled himself at Mondoun's feet and succeeded in knocking the witch doctor off balance.

Mondoun howled with rage and kicked Noel. "Get him, you fools!"

The more Noel moved the more strength returned to him.

Noel scrambled awkwardly aside, unable to dodge the pirates who reached for him. They dragged him upright, rougher than they needed to be. Noel looked around frantically for Leon and saw him holding Neddie by his collar, knife upraised. The child was white-faced with terror, too frozen to struggle. His golden curls shone soft and tender. That small, innocent throat was exposed, vulnerable. Leon ripped open the child's jacket and shirt, baring his chest. Neddie gulped and stood trembling, his enormous blue eyes riveted to the dagger above him.

Fear put extra volume into Noel's voice as he roared, "Leon! Are you crazy? Get away from that boy!"

Leon jerked around as though struck, and their gazes locked across the crowded room. Noel made no attempt to hide his disgust, and Leon's face darkened with rising color. His expression grew defensive, then sulky. His fingers twisted harder in the boy's collar, but Noel's glare grew hotter. In that moment he didn't care how much the pirates twisted his arms. He had forgotten Mondoun. He had forgotten everything but this twisted, disgusting, contemptible wretch duplicated from him by anomalies in the time stream. That Leon would go this far, would sink this low, would stoop to the senseless, cold-blooded murder of an innocent child on behalf of a superstitious ritual he didn't even personally believe in, was to Noel the ultimate, conclusive proof that Leon didn't deserve to exist. To let Leon continue to rampage through time and history, destroying everything he came in contact with, was as bad as letting a rabid animal terrorize a neighborhood.

Noel abandoned the pity he had always felt for Leon. He looked into the narrow face, the chiseled features that were so like his own—he still felt a slight shock every time the two of them came face-to-face—and he was sickened by what he saw.

"Don't look at me like that," said Leon, his voice shaking. He snarled, fury building in his silver eyes. "Don't look at me like that!"

Noel didn't intend to argue with him this time. He was past arguing, past trying to reform this sociopathic mutant. Coldly he said, "Let the boy go."

Leon's eyes widened. His fingers released the boy. Sobbing, Neddie wrenched free and scuttled for a corner.

"Leon, you fool!" shouted Mondoun, eyes blazing. He lifted his arms, and heat poured up from the trapdoor. The orange light intensified. "*Con—*"

"Shut up," said Noel, turning his head to glare at the priest. "I've had enough of your spells and your human sacrifices."

"You dare speak against the dark gods!" shrieked Mondoun. "You pathetic worm, what do you know of their power and—"

"LOC, activate," said Noel. He glared at Mondoun, ignoring the pressure the pirates were exerting on his arms. On his wrist, the LOC came on with a steady pulsing of blue light.

With startled murmurs, some of the men backed up.

"You will not use that here!" said Mondoun furiously. "I do not permit it."

"You don't command it, pal," said Noel defiantly. "You don't command me either."

Mondoun threw powdered herbs in Noel's face, making him sneeze and cough. A wave of dizziness swept him. The room tilted on its axis, and Noel knew he had inhaled some kind of drug. He fought its effects desperately, shaking his head in an effort to clear it. His ears were buzzing.

Mondoun started chanting, but Noel refused to give up. His tongue felt thick and clumsy, but he managed to say, "LOC, access reference file 110011. Greek Mythology, specifically gods. Project holograms."

"Silence him!" roared Mondoun.

One of the pirates clamped a hand over Noel's mouth. Noel bit his palm and with a howl of pain the man backhanded him across the mouth.

The blow made Noel's head ring. It nearly knocked him unconscious, but it also knocked away the effects of the drug. The bitter taste of blood from his cut lip helped finish clearing his head.

Before him, three white figures shimmered in midair. They were ghostly transparent because there wasn't a hologram reception screen to support the projection, but Noel had counted on that.

The pirates fell silent. They backed away from the three figures, shimmering in pale, knee-length chitons, laurel wreaths crowning their heads. One figure—Noel thought it was supposed to be Zeus—raised his right arm. His lips moved in the welcome to Mt. Olympus speech that was the prelude to an educational tour through the Hall of Ancient History in the museum wing of the Time Institute, but Noel had no intention of projecting sound to go with his apparition.

The two slaves dropped to their knees and pressed their foreheads to the floor in obeisance. The pirates looked uncertain; some crossed themselves in a sudden need for the religious training of their childhood.

"The *Rada* have come," said one reverently.

Others whispered, "The *Rada*. The gods of white magic."

"Shame to you, Baba," said another. "You did not tell us this man Noel Kedran is a *Hongoun*."

Mondoun's eyes flashed in anger. "He is no priest of the white gods. He is no—"

"Why does he then command such *loas*?"

Mondoun compressed his lips. He glared at Noel, who again avoided eye contact. Something powerful beat at Noel's mind. It sounded like rushing water, like thunder, like voices. He did his best not to listen. He could not, *must not* be caught in another spell.

"These are deceptions," said Mondoun. "They are not true *loas*. True *loas* would enter you. These are nothing but tricks. Look at how thin they are. Look at how they barely move. You need not fear something so insignificant."

"LOC," said Noel angrily, "enhance projection color. Replay recorded data sequence of Roman auxiliary legions marching. Specifically Gauls and Spaniards. Use foreshorted projection angle. Overlay harpies, and project sound."

"Silence him!" commanded Mondoun, but it was too late.

"Now," said Noel.

The cadenced tramping of feet started softly, then swelled in volume. A Roman trumpet blew, and many of the pirates jumped in startlement. Zeus and his two companions vanished, and an army poured into the room, dissolving as though the soldiers simply sank into the floor, with endless numbers coming in through the walls. Tall and gaunt, the Gauls strode along with long braided hair swinging about their shoulders, fierce, ragged mustaches streaked from the sun, animal skins obscuring their breastplates, protective leather straps hanging to their knees over their tunics, short swords clanking in scabbards at their sides, leather sandals tramping. They made the very floor shake, and just as the pirates began to relax a fraction and accept them as harmless apparitions, an earsplitting screech sent most of them cowering.

Half woman and half bird, the harpy was one of the most frightful inventions of Greek mythology. This speciman's long black hair blew in wild tangles about a woman's contorted face. Wings that nearly spanned the room flapped strongly, and the harpy swooped at them with wicked talons slashing. A dreadful stench filled the air, and with screams men exited the cabin despite Mondoun's attempts to stop them.

"LOC, project harpy outside," said Noel, and the monster sailed through the wall and outside into the storm after the terrified pirates.

Smug, Noel couldn't help but laugh at Mondoun. The witch doctor looked foolish and inept now, standing there with his followers scattered, his painted body ridiculous rather than frightening, his wig and hat askew.

"Cancel projection," said Noel, still grinning. The marching legions faded. He cocked his head at Mondoun. "Well, Baba, looks like you may be out of a job. Your days of voodoo evangelism on this ship are over."

Mondoun was breathing so hard he trembled. He stood erect, his body stiff and straight. His eyes held hatred as well as shock. "You mock what you do not understand. You are weak. All *Hongouns* are weak. You are no match for me."

"Hey," said Noel sharply, keeping the amused scorn in his voice to shock the man back into reality. "Drop this *Bocor* business. Anyone can pretend to call up ghosts and spirits, if they know the right tricks."

"Not tricks," said Mondoun furiously. "Not tricks. This is the true way of the gods." In the trapdoor, the orange light was growing dim. He raised his arms as though to commence another incantation.

Noel shook his head. "I said to forget it. The mumbo-jumbo isn't—"

In a blur of movement, Mondoun snatched up a dagger from his paraphernalia and threw it at Noel. Caught off-guard, Noel knew even as he bent his knees and twisted, throwing himself to one side, that he was too slow. While he urged his body to move faster, he was furiously scolding himself for having been so careless. He should have realized Mondoun was desperate enough to try anything. His training instructors and fellow travelers had always warned him that he was inclined to be too reckless, too impulsive for his own good. Now it was too late to agree with them, too late to tell himself that he shouldn't have gotten so cocky.

Then from his right, Leon barreled into him with a force that hurt. The impetus knocked Noel aside hard enough to send him sprawling. He caught himself on his hands and knees, skidding enough to catch some splinters on the rough wooden floor. Above him, Noel heard Leon grunt, then his duplicate was falling on top of him despite Noel's scramble to get out of the way.

Tangled beneath Leon's body, Noel glimpsed Mondoun climbing down through the trapdoor. Determined not to let Mondoun get away and regroup his shaken men, Noel squirmed free from Leon's weight and scrambled up in pursuit. But a wave of unexpected weakness washed through him, as though someone had switched off his energy. Noel found himself sagging to his knees, feeling curiously winded and light-headed.

He hadn't been wounded. The knife had missed him completely, thanks to Leon.

That's when he fully comprehended what had happened. Feeling cold, Noel turned but he already knew what he would see.

Leon lay on the floor behind him, breathing hard. The haft of the dagger protruded from the left side of his chest, heart-high. Mondoun's aim had been true enough. If Leon's heart was where it belonged, he would have been dead by now.

If he hadn't pushed me out of the way, thought Noel numbly, *I would be dead by now.*

Still, the wound was serious enough. A crimson stain was spreading rapidly across Leon's shirt. Blood frothed at his lips. He coughed, and the wheezing, rasping sound jerked Noel from his stunned immobility.

He gripped Leon's shoulders and lifted him as gently as he could to a sitting position to help him breathe.

"It got you in the lung," he said. "It's in deep, all the way to the handle."

Leon's pale gray eyes sought Noel's dark ones. His face was the color of bread dough. A sheen of sweat filmed it. He tried to speak, but couldn't.

"Easy," said Noel. "Don't talk."

As he spoke, he tightened his grip on Leon's shoulders, too shocked to know yet what he felt. Scant minutes ago, he had wished Leon dead and gone. Now it seemed he would have his wish.

The thought brought a lump to his throat. "Not like this," he whispered aloud.

Leon seemed to understand what he was thinking. He shuddered in Noel's grip and coughed up more blood. Real blood. Noel wiped it away. Leon closed his eyes. "Always wanted me . . . dead."

"Not dead," said Noel quickly, his voice sounding queer. "Just gone. Back to where you came from."

Leon stretched his lips in a ghastly attempt at a smile. "Define . . . death . . . in any other . . . way. Hate me. Want me dead."

"Oh, hell!" Noel tore off one of Leon's sleeves and began ripping it into strips. "Just shut up. You can't talk with a knife in your lung."

"Want . . . me dead. True."

"No."

Leon gripped his arm and glared at him. *"True!"* Then he started coughing again.

"You idiot," said Noel helplessly. "Be still and don't talk. We can't argue now."

Leon let his head slump back. His lids drooped, but with an effort he forced them open again. "Can't . . . argue later."

"You're not dying," snapped Noel, checking his back to see if the dagger had gone all the way through. It hadn't. He swallowed, knowing that he had to draw the dagger out, knowing that doing so might finish killing Leon.

Noel's hands were shaking. He paused a moment, trying to pull himself under control. It was like seeing himself injured, like watching himself die. Yet there was more to it than that. He realized he had begun to accept Leon's existence, no matter how much he resented it. To watch that existence ending was more than he had courage for.

Lady Pamela came up to them in a rustle of silk and petticoats. She touched Noel's shoulder, and he jumped violently, his heart thudding.

"I did not mean to startle you," she said.

Noel didn't answer. He propped Leon against a sea chest and stripped a blanket off the bunk. Dipping into the water pail, he gave Leon a drink, then dropped the dipper into the bucket with a splash.

"This is our chance to escape these wicked creatures," said Lady Pamela. "I pray you, sir, let us go now, while there is rain and darkness to cover our escape."

Noel glanced at her. For a moment she seemed a stranger to him. Then her features came into focus, and he met her green eyes. For the first time she looked genuinely frightened. Neddie clung to her skirts like a limpet.

"I must help him," said Noel.

She frowned. "In God's name, why? Brother or not, he is surely a blackguard and a murderer. He would have slaughtered this child had you not intervened. He is a willing participant in all the evil that has been done here."

"He saved my life."

As he spoke, Noel realized he was acting as though Leon had somehow redeemed himself. He should know better. Leon had been acting in his own self-interests, since without Noel he couldn't exist. Yet, Noel had never seen Leon risk his own neck before.

Unsure, he glanced down and saw Leon's eyes were slitted open, watching him. They glittered, dark with pain, unreadable.

Noel gripped Leon's hand. "Do you feel pain, real pain?"

Lady Pamela gasped before Leon could answer. "What kind of daft question is that? I fear you have lost your reason. Brother or not, he is not worth this—"

"Quiet!" said Noel roughly. "Leon, answer me. Do you feel pain?"

A strange, thoughtful expression appeared on Leon's face. Almost dreamily he said, "I have felt your pain. I feel your grief. Odd . . . hatred so hot it burns me, yet . . . sorrow? Why?"

"Never mind about me," said Noel. "I've got to know how much you can feel by yourself before I try to pull out the dagger."

Leon's eyes widened in alarm. "Don't kill me!"

He started coughing again, a violent spasm that left him exhausted and barely conscious. Worriedly, Noel realized he could delay no longer. Setting his hand upon the hilt, he bit his lip until he tasted blood, then drew out the dagger as smoothly and steadily as he could. Leon's back arched with it. His lips drew back from his teeth, but he did not scream.

The blade emerged, glistening red, and Noel threw it down before his nerveless fingers could drop it. Leon collapsed, blood everywhere. Noel hastily made a pad and bandaged it in place. It soaked through and he applied another, sweating and feeling so light-headed he wasn't sure if he could hold himself together.

It's not me who's dying, he thought. But he wasn't quite sure. He'd never been sure.

He shared none of Leon's pain, and the weakness he'd felt earlier had dissipated. Yet he hovered there, not knowing what else he could do, wishing for the first time that Leon had a LOC of his own. The mechanisms were equipped with emergency medical assistance. Noel had long since used his up. But he could use his LOC for other things.

He glanced at Lady Pamela, hesitating only briefly. She had already seen the computer work.

"LOC, activate."

His wristband came to life, growing warm about his wrist. "Working."

"Scan Leon," said Noel. "Run diagnostic checks on him. Make recommendations for treatment commensurate with technology of this century."

The LOC's steady pulse of light flickered. Noel watched it worriedly. Either the parameters he'd set were too strict, or something was interfering with it again. It flickered again, and its light grew dim. His heart sank.

"LOC," he said sharply. "Are you experiencing power loss?"

"Negative."

He almost managed to drag in a full breath. However, he didn't feel reassured. The last time the LOC acted like this, Mondoun had used it for a transmitter.

"Hurry," he said. "What can I do for Leon?"

"Blood pressure is—"

"Stop!" said Noel. "I don't want medical stats. Just tell me what to do for him."

"Is it a spirit you speak to?" asked Lady Pamela fearfully. "Does this familiar riding your wrist appear only in the form of light?"

Glancing at her frightened face, Noel snorted. "Oh, for God's sake. It's only a—" He stopped himself, his training reasserting itself. He must not tamper with events; he must not attempt to educate or advance people in considering ideas ahead of their time. "Witchcraft," he said thinly. "That's exactly right. You've seen enough of it tonight, surely?"

She drew back, her face so pale it looked bloodless.

He turned away, hoping she would stop interrupting, yet he regretted pandering to the ridiculous superstitions of this era.

"LOC! Dammit, answer me."

The LOC flashed brightly. It was now much hotter than usual on his wrist. "Anomaly warning."

Noel froze, his fingers digging into Leon's wrist instead of taking his pulse. "Specify."

"Anomaly warning."

"*Specify!* Is safety-chain programming operating? Are we about to end time course? Dammit, LOC, answer me!"

"Anomaly warning," said the LOC, flashing rapidly. It was so hot now on Noel's wrist he jerked in pain. Leon flinched too, yet did not awaken. "Anomaly . . . warn . . . ing. Re . . . ceiv. . . ing . . . trans . . . mis . . . sion . . . *attempts.*" The LOC's toneless voice had been slowing progressively, then without warning it speeded up to almost a staccato. "Limiter malfunction. Limiter malfunction. Warning retrograde one, zero, zero, zero—"

"Stop!" commanded Noel, smelling something burning, afraid it was shorting out. "Deactivate immediately."

The LOC shut off, and its normally clear sides looked smoky as though some of its optic fibers had indeed burned up. Noel's wrist hurt with increasing urgency. He unstrapped the LOC gingerly and peeled it off. A crimson burn mark encircled his wrist. Already the flesh was swelling. He winced and put the LOC on his right wrist.

"Dance with the devil, and you will prosper at first," said Lady Pamela righteously, "but eventually he turns on all his servants."

"Oh, thank you," said Noel with exasperation. "That's really very helpful, Lady Pamela."

He rose to his feet, and she backed away from him with her hand protectively on Neddie's shoulder. Before Noel could speak, a shudder ran through the ship. She lurched violently, and Noel lost his footing. He went rolling, the chairs tumbling over him along with Captain Miller's small collection of books and a brass sextant that thumped his skull hard enough to make his head ring.

Slamming into the far wall, Noel heard the ship moan. She struggled to rise, her timbers creaking with the strain, and came upright slowly. Noel made it to his feet, and the ship lurched again, hurling him in the opposite direction. He heard a crashing rip as though the bottom was being chewed from the ship, and they were flung down again.

She pitched violently, and water sloshed over the deckhouse heavily enough to run into the cabin beneath the door.

"What is happening?" cried Lady Pamela.

Noel struggled along the canted floor toward Leon, who'd been thrown beneath an overturned table. The lanterns were swinging wildly from the ceiling beams. The coals in the brazier spilled out and caught fire. Noel changed directions and scrambled for the water pail, only to find it overturned and empty. The ship tilted even farther, groaning like a dying beast. Water boomed outside as though the waves were trying to cave in the hull. Noel seized the bucket of sand that had been supporting the brazier and threw it over the flames, smothering them.

Only then did he meet Lady Pamela's frantic eyes. "I think we've run aground," he said, panting.

Neddie broke from her hold. "Mama!" he shouted. He ran for the door and wrenched it open just as another wave hurled itself over the ship. Water gushed over Neddie, knocking him back into the cabin. Noel grabbed the sputtering child by one ankle and dragged him to safety.

Rain and wind came lashing into the cabin, blowing out the lanterns, and plunging them into darkness. The ship settled lower. She was no longer pitching with the waves. Keeled sharply over on her right side, she groaned and broke inside. Noel heard screaming in the distance.

"We're aground, all right," he said grimly, thinking of the LOC's earlier announcement that the *Plentitude* was destined to go down. "And I think we're sinking."

CHAPTER 8

Sinking or not, this was not the time to stand around dithering. Noel groped his way across the slope of the floor until he found Leon. He slung his duplicate across his shoulder in a fireman's lift, trying to be gentle although there was no time.

Lady Pamela fought Neddie, who was struggling to break free from her and screaming for his mother. Noel joined them and gripped the boy's shoulder.

"Your mother will be all right," he said, shouting over the crash of the waves outside. More water gushed in, nearly knocking them off their feet. "You stick close to us. Can you swim?"

Neddie twisted away and ran for the door. "I've got to find her."

"Neddie, no!" cried Lady Pamela, trying to run after him, but Noel grabbed her wrist.

"Stay with me," he said. "Can *you* swim?"

"No, of course not," she said frantically. Outside a bolt of lightning struck close. She flinched and crossed herself. "Dear God in heaven, have pity on us!"

Noel shook her hard. "Pull yourself together," he said sharply. "You're an intelligent woman. I think you have considerable courage. Now's the time to use it. If you panic, you'll drown for sure out there. Hang on to my hand, and do as I tell you. All right?"

She made no answer. He was close enough to sense her shaking. He shook her again. "Pamela, dammit, do you understand what I've said to you?"

"I—I cannot trust you."

"You must!" he shouted. "Now, come on!"

Grasping her icy hand, he led her out into the fury of the storm. The wind's force nearly knocked him off his feet, and Lady Pamela staggered into him with a cry. Her hair streamed out from her head. Her long skirts billowed and snapped against her.

That unwieldy dress, Noel realized, would get her killed. She couldn't swim in such a garment. Right now, hampered by petticoats and a farthingale, she could barely walk in it.

He pushed her to the lee side of the poop, where they found a slight respite from the wind, and drew his dagger. Before she realized what he was about, he slashed at her skirts, cutting them off her.

She slapped him hard. "What are you doing? Have you gone mad?"

Ignoring her, he slashed through the lacings that held the whalebone framework supporting her petticoats. It fell to her feet, and she stood shivering in long linen pantalets and stockings, the ragged ends of her dress bodice fluttering at her waist.

"Take off your shoes!" he shouted at her.

She glared at him without moving, her face a pale blur in the lash of wind and rain.

"Pamela, take off your shoes!"

She kicked them off, then pulled out a hard, flat, triangular-shaped object from inside her bodice and hurled it at his head. Noel ducked barely in time.

"Have my stomacher as well, you scurvy-ridden knave! Have my ear bobs. Have my—"

He gripped her arm and held her pinned against the side of the cabin. "Shut up, damn you! Hysterics won't—"

"Hysterics?" She laughed wildly. "The ship is sinking, and even as I face my death you seek to strip me naked for all to see. Will you ravish me in public as well? Do you have time before the ship slides beneath the waves forever?"

Her accusations were irrational, the product of fear rather than malice, but they angered him just the same. Not trusting himself to argue with her, he tightened his hold on Leon's body weighing his shoulder down and yanked her away from the scant shelter.

"Come on!"

She stumbled after him, trying to pull free of his grip. "Let me go. I must find Lady Mountleigh and the child. We must say our prayers before we die."

Noel was finding it hard to keep his balance on the canted deck, and Leon's weight plus Lady Pamela's struggles did not help. A wave crashed over the gunwales, curling like a great, slobbering monster. It slammed him to his knees and swept Leon from his hold. Choking and spluttering, Noel released her and scrambled after his duplicate.

He managed to grab Leon's ankle just before his unconscious twin was swept overboard. Panting, Noel pulled Leon back to safety and looked around for Lady Pamela. All the lanterns had long since been extinguished. The only illumination came from the lightning bolts, and they were too irregular and too brief to be useful.

"Pamela!" he shouted with all his might. Squinting against the pounding rain, he cupped his hands to his mouth and called her name again.

From far away below deck he could hear faint screams of despair, and he knew the slaves were drowning. The poor wretches were chained down there, helpless against the water pouring in through the hole in the ship's hull. He doubted any of the pirates would bother to unchain them.

Noel swore to himself, then acted. He knew that he could not ignore those cries for help and live with himself.

Swiftly he knelt by his duplicate and shook his uninjured shoulder. "Leon! Leon, wake up! *Leon!*"

Leon did not stir. His skin was cold and wet to the touch. Only a faintly beating pulse in his throat told Noel that he was still alive.

Noel cut a short length of line from the rigging and used it to tie Leon to the base of one of the masts. At least now his duplicate was in no danger of being swept overboard. It seemed that fate must have surely befallen Lady Pamela, for she had not reappeared.

If she could have set aside her fear and trusted him, she'd still be alive. Her drowning was so senseless, so unnecessary. Noel was swept by fatigue and a sense of defeat, but he shook them off and made his way below. There, he found himself in a hellish situation.

All was chaos. Water gushed knee-deep, rising rapidly. Filth and bilge swirled in it. The stench nearly choked him. Rats twittered and squeaked from every available cranny and beam; others swam desperately. A handful of pirates splashed about in the gloom, some holding candles aloft, others blundering blindly. They were breaking open floating crates and smashing barrels, seeking what bits of loot they could stuff in their pockets before abandoning ship. The naked greed in their faces, the indifference to the plight of the shrieking slaves who were waist-deep in water at that end of the hold, infuriated Noel.

He grabbed the first pirate he encountered and yanked the man bodily away from the contents of a crate. "Where are the keys to the shackles?" he asked.

The man twisted like an eel in his hands. It was Natty Gumbel, scrawny and drenched, with his white, sightless eye staring at nothing. His other glared at Noel without recognition, being filled with desperation and avarice.

"Let me go, ye pox-ridden devil!" he shouted. "This loot be mine."

Noel glanced at the contents of the crate and saw that it held cups and saucers packed in straw: Lady Mountleigh's china service for her new home.

Noel shook Gumbel until the man's teeth chattered. "You're risking your life for teacups?" he shouted incredulously. "Are you crazy? Get a grip on yourself and look at what you're doing."

Natty Gumbel squirmed harder and tried to kick Noel's shins. "Let me go. Let me go! There be plenty fer ye. Take it, then."

Noel shook him again. "Forget your damned looting! Where are the keys for the prisoners?"

Gumbel blinked and finally seemed to recognize him. "Dunno. *Dunno!*"

There wasn't time to argue with him. Noel gave him a shove that toppled him over. Gumbel splashed around, knocking away the rats that tried to clamber from the water onto his shoulders. Righting himself, the pirate scurried away.

Noel approached another man filling a sack with swag. Without a word, this one swung a dangerous fist. Noel ducked, and the man splashed away.

The imprisoned officers of the *Plentitude* were chained down here as well. One of them yelled, "God rot your cowardly souls, all of you!"

Noel splashed by them, refusing to meet the looks of contempt and fear hurled at him. Squeezing himself into the stern, he climbed up to the gunnery platform. Several cannons had broken free of their moorings and had smashed through the hull when the ship ran aground. Water poured in around them. A lit lantern still swung from a ceiling beam, casting a feeble glow of illumination over the area. Noel didn't know what it was doing there since it was folly to leave fire of any kind near the powder kegs. However, in these conditions, with powder kegs floating in all directions like flotsam, there seemed little danger of an explosion.

He unhooked the lantern and held it aloft, squinting as it reflected off the filthy water that was still rising. There wasn't much time left before the entire hold flooded.

On the wall, he found at last what he was looking for. The long poles used for ramming wad into the cannons hung on their brackets. Beneath them was a hatchet.

With a snort of satisfaction, Noel plucked it down and waded back to the prisoners.

He hacked at the chains of the ship's officers first, striking sparks, but finally breaking a link. The men yelled encouragement and went to work, worrying the chain apart and then unthreading it from their shackles.

Noel hurried over to the slaves. Unlike the officers, these prisoners were chained individually. Some of them were in water too deep to make a blind blow with the hatchet safe.

He didn't want to cut off someone's foot by mistake.

Realizing that he was trying to free them, the Africans reached out imploring hands and called to him in their own tribal tongues. His translator deciphered some of it. Noel swallowed, feeling bleak and inadequate. He couldn't help them all.

Those whom he freed helped in turn by lifting the individuals trapped in the deepest water, thus exposing their chains where he could strike with the hatchet. The weapon was growing blunted with every blow. He hacked as fast as he could. Some of the links snapped readily; others refused no matter what he did.

And there was so little time. He never forgot that Leon was up there, tied to the mast, helpless and unconscious, probably dying alone in the storm. The thought twisted Noel up inside, made him feel hollow and afraid. He hadn't expected to ever worry about Leon. But he found himself pitying Leon all over again, although he didn't want to. He knew Leon's reasons for saving his life were selfish ones, but that didn't change the fact that he would have been dead now—a dagger through his heart—had Leon not intervened.

The ship shuddered, and with a fearsome snapping of timbers, she broke apart yet more. Water rose at an alarming rate, and the cries of the Africans hushed abruptly as though they realized they had run out of time. Some of the freed ones darted about frantically, seeking the way out. Noel knew he couldn't stay down here longer.

He handed the hatchet to a tall man with ceremonial scars who still stood in chains. The man took the weapon without a word, but in his eyes lay somber acknowledgment of Noel's help. Noel headed for the exit. Some of the Africans were so weak and ill they could not walk. They sank down in the water with moans of despair. Others followed Noel grimly, ignoring their debilitated condition in the quest for freedom.

At the stairs he stood aside and gave several of them a helping boost, letting them climb ahead of him into the storm. When he emerged onto the deck, he found them waiting, perhaps a dozen of all ages and sizes, men and women, naked, starved, and desperate. They knelt to him, bowing deeply.

"Thank you, bwana."

"Thou art our lord, bwana."

"We serve thee, bwana."

Noel's throat tightened. He shook his head. "I'm not your master. Save yourselves. Don't waste time bowing to me."

They straightened, but they did not flee. Across the deck, he glimpsed the officers climbing over the gunwales, helping each other. He saw also a woman's skirts billowing in the wind. Relief and exasperation filled him. Why the devil had Lady Pamela gone off to put on another dress? Didn't she understand she couldn't swim in those damned clothes?

Then he saw the boy and knew it was Lady Mountleigh instead of the girl. He bowed his head, so tired he could barely stand. The Africans crowded closer. Some of them took his hands and pressed his palms to their foreheads like dogs nuzzling for affection.

Noel roused himself. He couldn't stop now. These Africans still needed his help. Having freed them from the hold, now he was responsible for getting them off the ship. One of them, he noticed, was the scrawny, half-grown boy who carried himself like a prince, the boy who'd been present at Mondoun's ceremony. The LOC had foretold this boy's future as the leader of a slave uprising on one of the islands. If nothing else, Noel had to get him safely off ship.

"Come," he said to him and gestured.

They streamed after him like half-seen shadows in the night, struggling against the wind that made Noel stagger. He found Leon still tied to the mast and knelt to untie him.

"What the devil are these slaves doing topside?" asked an arrogant English voice.

Noel glanced up and saw a shape standing over him. He couldn't make out the features, but he figured it was one of the officers he'd just freed.

"Did you set them loose?" demanded the man.

Those cold, incredulous tones infuriated Noel. He rose to face the man.

"Yes, I freed them, just like I freed you."

"You had no right. They're valuable cargo—"

Noel sprang at the man and socked him in the jaw. The man staggered back, and Noel went after him, seizing him by the coat front.

"Cargo!" he shouted furiously. "They're people. Living human beings. If they stay down there they'll drown."

"You have no right to dispose of our cargo," said the man implacably. He knocked Noel's hands away and shook out his clothes. "I order you to—"

"Go to hell."

"You can't set untrained slaves loose on these islands. Where's your sense of responsibility?"

"My *what*?" shouted Noel.

"Responsibility. They'll cause all sorts of problems among the others. The planters will be furious with us."

Noel couldn't believe he was having this conversation in the middle of a hurricane with the ship sinking under them. "Why don't we see if they even survive first?" he said sarcastically.

"You don't understand—"

"No, *you* don't understand. If they stay aboard they will drown. They will die. I've given them a chance to live."

"What the devil does that matter?"

"My God!" exploded Noel, clenching his fists. "Aren't they better off alive than dead? What's wrong with you?"

The man sputtered. "The insurance, my good man. The insurance."

"What insurance? What are you talking about?"

"If they drown in the hold, we can collect for our losses. If they escape, we have no coverage."

Noel couldn't believe it. "They aren't teacups or bolts of cloth. They're people!"

"They're slaves."

Noel, trained in ancient history, was familiar enough with the institution of slavery. But the Roman culture had been a sophisticated, fairly humane one. Some slaves had been wealthy, influential individuals. They had certain rights, certain obligations, certain rules that they had to live by. But they weren't considered cattle. And they certainly weren't drowned just so their master could collect on his insurance.

"Now herd them back below deck where they belong," said the man.

"The hell I will," said Noel.

He sprang at the man, who raised his arms to guard himself against another blow. Instead, Noel seized him by his coat and propelled him across the deck and over the gunwale by sheer impetus. He heard a yell, then a splash, and smiled to himself in grim satisfaction.

He turned to go back to the mast, and saw that the Africans had untied Leon. Noel waved at them and stepped forward. Lightning forked the sky. It struck the top of the mainmast and blue electricity sizzled down the pole. The Africans screamed and scattered, and beneath the deafening roar of thunder Noel heard a mighty crack of splitting wood.

He looked up and saw the mast sway. Horrified, he yelled a warning, but the thing was already straining at its cables. Some of the lines snapped with a vicious twanging and whipped through the air. The mast leaned. The shrouds broke, and Noel hastily ducked. With a terrible groan, the mast came down.

Rooted in place by sick fascination, Noel realized he was in its path but he could not move. It fell slowly, majestically, its progress delayed by the remaining forestays snapping one by one. It dragged down with it a sweep of tattered sails and rigging, the complex but ordered system of ropes, pulleys, sails, halyards, and spars all chaotic and tangled now.

Then the slow, groaning progress of the mast halted, held impossibly by a final quivering line. Noel stared up at it like a child, fascinated despite the danger.

It had stopped, he told himself. His eyes widened, and he drew in a sweet deep breath. He even grinned to himself and wiped the rain from his face.

The ship heeled over with a loud groan, going nearly flat on her starboard side. The shift put too much strain on the line. It broke, and the mast crashed down. Shaken from the spell that had held him, Noel tried to run now that it was too late. Like a toppling sequoia, the mainmast snapped off a lesser mast that bounced and rolled, missing Noel by scant feet. Losing his balance on the steeply sloped deck, he went sprawling and came up hard against a stack of barrels lashed to the deck. Stunned, he tried to scramble on, frantic now and cursing himself for having stood flat-footed until it was too late.

A tackle block as large as his head thudded into the deck next to him, and heavy rigging hit him like a blow, its weight forcing him down and pinning him.

He struggled to roll clear, but the rope held him tangled. The mainmast hit with a force that jarred the deck. The whole ship seemed to be caving in. He was smothering. More things fell on him, pinning him, crushing him. He couldn't breathe. He couldn't see. The ship was still tilting, as though she was at last being sucked beneath the raging sea.

Down with all hands, thought Noel blearily. It seemed the LOC's prediction was going to be even truer than he'd originally suspected.

And then he was drowning.

CHAPTER 9

Heat brought Noel back from the long darkness of nowhere. It baked him, making him increasingly uncomfortable and restless. For a long time he endured it, hovering on the edge of consciousness, but it was the trickle of sweat running into his eye that finally woke him up.

He opened his eyes, and the harsh glare of light made him squint painfully. He closed his eyes and sought to return to the safety of unconsciousness, but now his mind stirred and remembered. There had been the storm, the drums, the raging sea.

With a start, he pushed himself up. The world tilted dizzily about him, making him shut his eyes again. Finally, however, he eased them open and focused.

He sat on the beach. The white sand was strewn with the debris of planks, coconuts, dead birds, tree limbs, tangles of rope, barrel staves, articles of clothing, and shells scoured up from the bottom of the sea. The beach curved around the blue-green waters of the cove. The waves rippled in, meek and sun-kissed, as different from the gray, raging whitecaps of last night as possible.

The little harbor itself was empty. He squinted out at the blue horizon and saw no sails there. Gulls dipped and wheeled on the hot breeze, shrieking and fighting for the fish that had been washed up in the storm's violence and left stranded.

Noel frowned and ran his fingers through his sand-crusted hair. He was skinned and bruised. His mouth tasted of brine. He wore no clothing except the tattered remnants of his trousers. His left eye was swollen and puffy to the touch. The vision in that eye seemed a little blurred. His lungs hurt with every breath, as though he'd inhaled some water. He vaguely remembered the sensation of drowning. Obviously, however, the sea hadn't wanted him.

More memories returned to him. He staggered to his feet in sudden anxiety and looked around. "Leon?" he called.

Startled by his voice, the gulls flew up from the beach and wheeled out over the bay, fussing with their strident cries.

"Leon!"

He paused a moment, listening to the steady rush of the water, the breeze rustling in the palm trees that hadn't been uprooted by the storm. Out by the mouth of the bay, he could see a dark, rounded silhouette. He knew it was the hull of the *Plentitude,* three-quarters submerged and most likely a grave for those who had not managed to escape her final moments.

"Leon!"

His voice echoed into the jungle.

A flock of flamingoes flew over him and settled on the beach. The pink, stately birds strolled about, pecking curiously at the debris and dipping their heads into the surf. They showed no fear of him.

Noel glanced around and touched the Plexiglas bracelet on his right wrist. "LOC, activate."

He felt a responsive warmth from it on his skin before the circuits flashed to life.

"Working," said the LOC.

"What's the date?"

"June sixteenth, 1697."

He frowned. "No way, pal. Hurricanes don't blow themselves out that quickly. Not in a matter of hours. Try again."

"Is that a rhetorical question?"

"I didn't ask a question. I gave you a command. What is the date?"

The LOC pulsed a moment. "Incorrect response."

He thumped it with his finger. "Do you have sea water inside you?"

"Negative."

"Then what's the problem?"

"Restate question. What problem do you wish analyzed?"

Noel sighed and rubbed the back of his neck. He was hungry. His mouth had been shriveled by thirst. He was hot and sunburned and tired. Why the hell did the LOC have to act like this now?

Reminding himself that it was just a machine, however sophisticated, and efficient only if he was the same, Noel forced himself to concentrate.

"Let's start over."

"Working."

"You say that today's date is still June sixteenth, 1697."

"Affirmative."

"Are you malfunctioning in your present time counter?"

"Negative."

"What about the hurricane? How could it blow itself out in just a matter of hours? If it hit the mainland I could see it slowing down and dissipating, but not out here. It should still be raining, even if the winds were downgraded. I don't understand."

The LOC grew hotter on his wrist. "The velocity of wind was measured at seventy-two miles per hour. Although hurricanes are generally between seventy and one hundred thirty-five miles per hour, some—such as Hurricane Camille in 1969 and Hurricane James in 2114—can reach a force of almost two hundred."

"Yeah, so?"

"This storm did not maintain hurricane strength winds for more than two point seven hours. It did not develop a true circular rotation. By the time it reached Cuba shortly after dawn, it had dissipated into a heavy thunderstorm. Rainfall counts are—"

"Stop," said Noel. "You're saying we weren't in a hurricane?"

"Affirmative. Tropical storm is the correct designation, based on the—"

"Never mind," said Noel impatiently. He glanced at the glaring sun overhead. "It's what? About midday? Is safety-chain programming still running?"

The LOC flashed for several seconds but made no reply.

Noel thumped it. "LOC! Is safety-chain programming still running? Respond."

Nothing.

Alarm stirred in Noel. He couldn't afford to have the thing go haywire on him now. He needed it too much.

"Come on, LOC. Answer me."

Nothing.

"LOC!" he said sharply. "Locate Leon. Full scan. Is he alive?"

"Scan . . . ning," said the LOC.

Noel's heart sank. The malfunctions were increasing. For a while he'd thought the LOC might succeed in repairing the damage that had been done to it. But now those hopes were dashed. The LOCs were built to withstand considerable abuse, but they remained delicate pieces of complex technology. Not only had the LOC been dunked more than once into corrosive salt water, but it was probably beginning to experience stress fractures in its biochips. No one had ever been trapped in a closed time loop before. No one had ever stayed in the past this long before. No one had ever traveled on successive missions without returning to the present before. So who knew how long the LOC could hold up? Noel wasn't certain how many more times he could survive passing through the time vortex himself.

"LOC, buddy, you can't quit on me now," he said with a desperate break in his voice. It was so hot now on his wrist his skin was beginning to feel scorched. "Scan for Leon. Tell me if he's alive."

"Scan . . . ning . . . to . . . or . . . i . . . gin . . . p-p-p-point," droned the LOC.

"No! Not origin point," said Noel. "Not now. Unless there's an incoming message from origin point?"

"Af . . . firm . . . a . . . tive."

Noel gasped with hope. "Receive message!"

The LOC pulsed rapidly. "Mal . . . function." Its voice speeded up to normal, then got faster and shriller. "Malfunction. *Malfunction!*"

"Cancel! Deactivate!"

The LOC went dead. Noel's eyes stung with disappointment. He swallowed a lump in his throat and kicked the sand furiously. His friends at the Time Institute were still trying to reach him, still trying to get him back, yet as long as the LOC remained unable to establish a communications link there could be no return. He wasn't sure which was worse: having no contact signals from his own time or knowing they were trying but couldn't reach him.

He'd read about shipwrecked individuals withering away on desert islands, scanning the empty seas for rescue, sometimes even seeing a sail on the horizon only to watch it pass by unheeding of their plight. He'd read about loneliness, starvation, the slow, eventual madness.

Now, he knew what it was like to be alone, abandoned, without hope. He could not get home. His LOC was disintegrating. Even Leon—his mirror image, his hated nemesis whose very existence had been a constant chafing point—was now gone, probably dead. Perhaps some of the others had survived and had washed up on this island, but they were not of his kind, not of his century.

He hurt inside with a sudden, terrible ache. He crouched down and hugged his arms tightly around his knees, compressing himself in an effort to hold together.

But giving way to fear was like giving way altogether. If he ever let himself crumble completely, he did not think he could pull himself back.

Breathing harshly, he tipped his head to gaze at the sky, then forced his knees to straighten. He scanned the beach, then took a step, then another, making himself walk down to where the debris was the worst.

He began to search for survivors, muting his thoughts, refusing to acknowledge the fear gnawing holes in him.

"LOC," he said once.

It hummed sporadically, its light blinking dim.

"Assume disguise mode."

It did not respond.

He sighed, realizing that its molecular shift capability had been lost. He should have known that last night when he was using the LOC in full view of everyone and the LOC made no effort to disguise itself or to prevent him from utilizing technological terms that its programming was supposed to eliminate from the translator.

Perhaps he had finally succeeded in changing history irrevocably. Perhaps the time stream had closed, and the changes had become permanent. Perhaps his future was already gone, and the LOC's disintegration was indicative of that situation. Perhaps he himself would next begin to fade.

He no longer knew what to expect.

Grasping a tangle of rigging half-buried in the sand, he tugged it free and rolled it aside. He found a sea chest beneath it, lying upside down, its contents gone.

Wiping his face with a hand that smelled fishy and damp, Noel went on.

Some of the articles of clothing near the water proved to be people. He tugged them out—three Africans and a pirate with no ears and a string of perfectly matched pearls around his neck. All four were dead. Noel took off the pearls and tucked them in his pants pocket. As he did so, he glanced yet again at the merciless sun. He would have to dig graves soon.

Wearily he staggered on, following the curve of the beach.

A massive sea turtle crawled over the hot sand ahead of him, making her ponderous way back to the sea. He left her alone but tracked her path to the nest of freshly laid eggs that she'd left in the sand. His stomach rumbled with hunger, and he thought numbly that he'd have to think of feeding himself soon. But baby turtles weren't his idea of lunch.

To his left, something rustled in the jungle. Noel stared in that direction, but he saw nothing unusual among the thick undergrowth of shrubs and ferns. Ahead, and a bit inland, he could see the mangrove swamp that he'd blundered into . . . was it only last night?

Remembering the bats that had attacked him, he shivered. He didn't know what had become of Baba Mondoun, but he hoped the creep had drowned.

Turning to reverse his steps, Noel heard the rustle again. He stopped and listened to the wind rustling the palms. Bird calls, the soft burble of surf . . . nothing else. Yet he *had* heard something.

Now he felt the sensation of someone staring at him. His first instinct, as always, was to confront it. But Mondoun had made him cautious.

Longing for a weapon, he glanced around and picked up a piece of driftwood. A club was better than nothing.

"Skulking in the bushes, picking up sand fleas won't help you," he called out, hoping his voice sounded confident. "You might as well come out."

Nothing.

Noel grimaced to himself. On impulse he hurled the driftwood into the bushes where he'd last heard the noise.

A head popped up, then vanished. He saw the ripple of undergrowth and ran at it, scooping up another stick on the way. A corner of his mind was warning him that this could be another trap to lure him into the jungle, but he didn't care. He wasn't going to let himself be spooked by spies and strange noises.

Whoever it was didn't move very quickly. Noel gained easily. He made a flying tackle through a huge fern and knocked his quarry down. In the blur of struggle, he glimpsed black skin. Certain it was Mondoun, he let go as though burned. The other scrambled hurriedly into the thicket, but not before Noel glimpsed a skinny ankle rubbed raw by an iron shackle.

Picking himself up with a groan of weariness, Noel pursued his quarry again and caught him within a few steps. He dragged him out, shaking him just in case he had thoughts of putting up a fight.

The boy, however, was spent. Ashen-faced and trembling with fatigue, he lifted his scarred face to Noel's in silent entreaty. It was Kona Masi, the boy predicted to lead a slave uprising some day.

Noel's harsh grip gentled. He knelt by the panting boy and tried a smile.

"Hey, easy," he said while Kona gulped for breath. "Sorry I chased you. I didn't know who was spying on me."

The boy seemed to understand, for after a moment the thin shoulders relaxed. Kona looked less frightened and more resigned.

"Not spying," he said in English, his African accent soft and slurred. "Afraid. Hungry. Not enemy. Not fight."

"Sure," said Noel with another smile. "No fight. I'm looking for survivors. You want to help?"

"Leg hurt."

Noel was sure it did. The heavy shackle had made a horrible sore on the boy's ankle. The flesh was red and puffy with infection. Noel frowned with quick anger. Kona was a good-looking boy; his eyes were intelligent. Despite fear, filthiness, and the starvation that had worn him down to skin and bones, the abuse from his captors had not entirely broken his spirit. He still carried himself with pride. Perhaps he had been a prince in his own tribe. But even if he had been a goat herder, no one had the right to snatch him from his home and family and carry him off into slavery.

"Let's see what we can do for this," said Noel. He got up and took Kona's hand. "Come on."

Reluctantly the boy limped after him. Noel made him stand in the water, figuring the salt water would clean the wound better than anything else available. He tore off his pants leg to the knee and gently bandaged Kona's ankle. The boy winced but made no protest.

"That will help protect the wound until we can get this damned shackle off," said Noel. "It will still hurt, I'm afraid, but at least it won't get worse."

The taut set of Kona's mouth eased fractionally. "Is better."

Noel smiled. "Well, come on then. If I found you alive, maybe someone else survived too."

But Kona stood where he was and did not follow. Noel glanced back at him impatiently and gestured. Kona did not move.

"Last night, you save."

"Yeah, I did," said Noel. "Come on."

"Now you treat good. Is Kona your slave now?"

"No, you're not my slave," said Noel shortly.

Kona's eyes grew fierce. "Is smart to help slave. Keep property alive and strong. Property more valuable then."

Noel swung around to face him. "Look, kid, I don't own people."

"You are poor man?"

"No, I'm not poor. I don't believe people should own other people. You are valuable to yourself. I am valuable to myself. I didn't save you because I've got some sugar cane plantation around here and need workers. I saved you because you needed help. I hope you would do the same for me if things were reversed."

"You are white *bwana*. You no slave."

Bitterness caught Noel in the throat. "Oh, yeah, sure. I'm free as a bird. Only I'm stuck here on this little piece of sand the same as you, with no food in my gut and no way to get off."

He swung around and started walking. After a few moments, the jingle of the ring bolt on Kona's shackle told him the boy was following. Noel slowed his pace and let Kona catch up.

"If you get off," said Kona after a few moments, "where go?"

Noel's stride faltered. That was a very good question. What was he striving for? With his LOC malfunctioning so much it probably couldn't yank him through to another time again, what was the difference between this island and another?

"Exiled in paradise," he said aloud, gazing around at the blue waters and the white sand. "Other than the bats, this place isn't so bad."

Kona's thin face was so serious, Noel decided to forget about his own problems. "What about you?" he said. "If you could go anywhere, where would it be?"

Kona blinked as though the notion was new to him. After a long, thoughtful pause, he said slowly, "The gods have made a world that is very wide. I cannot choose."

"How about home?" asked Noel softly.

"Home?" Kona's face contorted with anger. He said something untranslatable and spat. "To be slave again in the kraal of my enemies? To wear scars of shame and crawl in dust? No home. No!"

Noel raised his brows in surprise. He hadn't realized African tribes made slaves of others. But it made sense. Man's inhumanity to man wasn't limited to race.

"Sorry," he said.

"Hungry," said Kona. "Let us hunt."

They took a break and ate juicy mangoes and the weird breadfruit that Noel didn't care for much. Although the juice had slakened his thirst somewhat, he knew that sooner or later they were going to have to enter the jungle and go to the spring. He dreaded venturing very far into the shadowy trees, however, and put it off.

"I'm going to walk on around the beach."

"Hunt people?"

"That's right."

Kona shrugged. "Why?"

"Because," said Noel, "I don't like surprises."

"Enemies?"

"Maybe. You remember Baba Mondoun?"

Kona shook his head.

"The *Bocor*," said Noel.

Fear flickered in Kona's face. He made a swift gesture to ward off evil.

"That's the one," said Noel. "I don't know if he's on this island or not, but I'd hate to bet that he went down with the ship. You stay here and collect coconuts and fruit. Don't go into the jungle. If Mondoun shows up, yell."

Kona said nothing. His eyes, however, darted nervously. Noel started to walk away, and Kona gripped his hand.

"No go!"

"I'll be back," said Noel, disengaging gently. "I have to look for someone."

"Seek enemies, good chance you find. Then fight. Then trouble."

"I'm not looking for my enemy," said Noel in a quiet voice. "I'm looking for . . . my brother."

He turned sharply and strode away, his jaw set and his eyes fierce with emotions he didn't want to acknowledge. Dammit, what was wrong with him that he should be so upset over Leon, who shouldn't even exist anyway? He ought to be rejoicing. It was a relief to be rid of his troublemaking duplicate at last.

Only, he wished Leon hadn't saved his life at the end. He felt guilty; he felt grateful. He didn't want to feel either emotion.

The west side of the island was rockier, with less of a beach. He saw cloth flutter in the breeze, and he quickened his pace. It was a flag, fashioned from a white linen handkerchief and a stick.

Noel turned around, scanning the beach and rocks. "Hello!" he called. "Hello!"

He saw a flash of gold hair in the sun, a glimpse of blue cloth. Noel headed into the rocks, climbing over shale and boulders in a scramble that brought him to a shallow recess in the rock face. It was shady here, damp and cold.

Neddie, gasping for breath, his face white with fear, crouched beside Lady Mountleigh. Her pale hair hung in limp hanks about her face. She had a purple bruise on one temple, and she looked unconscious.

"Please help us, sir," said Neddie in anguish. "Please have pity, sir, and don't kill us."

"I won't kill you," said Noel. "I'm not a pirate."

The boy's blue eyes dropped. A blush tinged his pale cheeks, and Noel saw him swallow convulsively. He gripped his mother's hand and said in a shaking voice, "I think she will die."

Noel crouched beside him. "Let's see. Move aside and give me room."

"Don't hurt her!"

Noel met the child's anxious eyes. He reminded himself that Neddie was only seven and had been through quite a shock. "I won't," he said. "But I need to check to see if she has any water in her lungs or if there are bones broken."

"She cast up a fearsome mess of salt water hours ago," said Neddie. "I was sick too."

"Good," said Noel. Ignoring the boy's chatter, he felt the woman's clammy limbs as gently as he could and listened to her breathing. It looked like the worst injury she'd suffered was the blow to her head.

He felt encouraged and scooped Lady Mountleigh up in his arms. She was short but plump. He staggered a bit under her weight, increased by her voluminous skirts, and began to pick his way carefully down through the rocks.

"Where are you taking her?" asked Neddie, skipping beside him. "Are there others alive? We don't want to be prisoners of the pirates again."

"I haven't seen any pirates," said Noel, puffing for breath already. His arms ached, and his knees felt rubbery. Having swallowed half the ocean last night, plus all the other ordeals he'd been through, left him in poor shape to be a hero. She weighed a ton, and was getting heavier all the time.

"Have you a pistol?" asked Neddie. "Have you a sword?"

"No."

"We must prepare a defense point. Perhaps we can salvage the guns from the ship. I can see the wreck out there. It wouldn't be far to swim."

Noel blinked sweat from his eyes. "Forget it."

"No, I'm an excellent swimmer," said Neddie. "The pirates will come back for their booty. We must defend ourselves and the women."

Hope rose sharply in Noel. "Lady Pamela is all right?"

Neddie's face fell. "I—I haven't seen her, in truth. I was speaking in general. There is Mama, after all."

Noel stubbed his toe on something and swore under his breath. His head was roaring. He wheezed for air and abruptly sank to his knees.

"Why are you stopping?" asked Neddie. "Your face is red. Are you tired? How far do you mean to carry her? She can't be left in the sun. It makes her head ache and will burn her skin. Will you—"

"For God's sake," said Noel in exasperation, catching his breath, "will you be quiet?"

There was a moment of injured silence while Neddie's face grew pinched and resentful. "You must not speak to me in that manner," he said in a haughty tone. "You are addressing your superior. You must give me respect."

"You have to earn respect, boy."

"No, I don't! I'm a Sinclair. I'm a gentleman. You're just a—"

Noel gripped the boy's wrist and shook him. "You can have your tantrums later. Right now your mother needs help. I can't carry her all the way around the beach, so we're going to have to build a shelter over her. Go gather all the palm fronds you can find that have been blown off the trees."

Neddie wrenched free. He turned red with anger, and his lip jutted out. "How dare you give me orders. You gather them. I am going to stay with Mama and protect her."

"Look, brat," said Noel. "You—"

"Bwana!" called Kona, limping hurriedly in his direction.

Neddie saw him and gasped. He gave Noel a shove and stood next to his mother, holding a piece of driftwood as a weapon.

"Relax," said Noel. "Kona's on our side."

"I shan't let that savage near my mother," said Neddie.

"Bwana," said Kona, limping up. "All well?"

"Yes," said Noel.

Neddie poked Kona with the stick. "Get away!"

Noel's temper snapped. He turned on the child and snatched the stick from Neddie's grasp. Breaking it across his knee, Noel flung the pieces away.

"Listen to me, you hypocritical little brat. Kona is not a savage. You won't treat him like one. You got that?"

Neddie's lip was jutting out again. It quivered. "You can't talk to me like that. My father will punish you."

"Your father's not here. Now if you want us to help you and your mother, you had better start mending your manners."

Neddie gulped. His blue eyes filled with tears, but he wouldn't let them fall. "I know how to deal with servants. Papa says one must be firm."

"Oh, yeah?" retorted Noel. He curbed the burning urge to give this brat a spanking. "Well, try this on for size. We aren't servants."

"Yes, of course you are."

"Nope. Specifically we aren't *your* servants."

"But—"

"No. Get it through your stupid, overprivileged skull right now, once and for all. We'll help you because we're nice guys and your mother is hurt. But we don't *have* to lift a finger on your behalf. And if you give me one more order in that snotty tone of yours, I'll smack your backside quicker than you can turn around."

Neddie's eyes widened. "You—you would strike me?"

Noel glared at him, although now that he had the upper hand his anger was dissipating rapidly. He wasn't going to let Neddie see that, however. "Yes, I would. Now you and Kona are going to build a shelter to give your mother some shade. Is that okay, Kona?"

The African nodded. "This woman bad hurt?"

"I don't know yet," said Noel. "I think she hit her head pretty hard. She probably has a concussion. She's too heavy to carry any farther, so we'll just have to take care of her here."

"Is dry here. Very hot."

Noel tried to hang on to his patience. They were both children, after all, although Kona was twice Neddie's size. Neddie sniffled and rubbed his eyes, and Noel sighed.

Without another word, he went off to gather the poles and the palm fronds. Kona watched him for a few minutes, then took over the actual construction.

"Thanks," said Noel. "Can you baby-sit for a while?"

Kona frowned. "Babee?"

"Baby-sit. Watch the kid and his mom. He's probably hungry too."

"Why does he not go and hunt for his mother?" asked Kona critically.

"Because no one has taught him how. He's not been raised like you, Kona. He's pretty helpless."

"Babee," said Kona smugly, lifting his chin.

Noel bit back a smile. "That's right."

"I watch."

"Thanks. I won't be long. I'll search the beach to the western tip of the island, then I'll come back."

Kona nodded, and Noel left with a sense of relief. Glancing back once, he saw that Neddie was watching Kona work like some kind of miniature lord surveying his kingdom, but at least the brat was quiet.

Well past the point where he found Neddie and his mother, Noel saw a body, a woman lying facedown. Noel's heart contracted. He ran to her and knelt.

The brown hair was dry now. Tangled with strands of seaweed and dusted with sand like glitter, it stirred softly in the breeze. He touched it and felt its silken texture. Beneath it, the curve of her skull was solid and still. Too still. He knew before he rolled her over and looked at her white, lifeless face.

Lady Pamela's green eyes would never flash again. Her incisive voice would never rap out orders. Her lovely, rather serious face would never again grimace with impatience or melt into a radiant smile. She lay there, looking small and defenseless in her undergarments.

Noel bowed his head, gripping her hand hard as though to recall her, wishing that he could reverse those hectic moments last night when he'd been too distracted to pay attention to her panic. If he'd been more patient, if he'd even bothered to tie a rope on her, she might be alive now.

But was she supposed to survive the storm?

He shook the question angrily away. The LOC had said she wasn't listed among the survivors. He had known from that moment that he couldn't save her. Yet it still hurt. He still felt like a failure.

For the first time in his career, he questioned the value of time travel. What good was it to know someone's future if you weren't allowed to save them? What kind of pathetic voyeurism was it to stand on the sidelines and watch someone fail or die, making recordings of the event for posterity, yet not helping?

Travelers justified their noninvolvement on the basis of the time paradox principle. Yet, although it was vital to protect the

future and not change it, what good did it really do to enter the
past? Had any research data collected by the historians done
any good? Had it solved any of the social problems of the
twenty-sixth century?

No.

Noel rose to his feet and stared bleakly at the horizon where
the sun was dropping toward the ocean. The waves glittered
like beaten copper. The warm breeze played on his back. His
face twisted with bitterness and he dashed his tears angrily
away with his hand.

He was tired of it, tired of himself, tired of what he stood
for. Maybe the anarchists were right and civilization had lasted
too long. Maybe it was time to let things fall to dust and
darkness.

He swallowed hard and watched the ocean, eternal, uncaring.
He felt like a fool.

CHAPTER 10

He found Leon half-buried beneath a tangle of boards and rope, someone's shoe, some water-logged books with the ink all washed off the pages, and a brass sextant that should have sunk to the bottom of the sea. Weary of death, Noel stared down at his duplicate and almost left him there. But if nothing else, Leon deserved a burial. Slowly Noel went to work shifting the junk off him.

When he pulled Leon out and rolled him over, Leon groaned.

Noel's heart stopped. He crouched there, his hands curiously frozen, and stared down at the pale, sunken features that were so like his own. Until now he hadn't let himself look closely at Leon. It was too much like seeing his own death.

But now . . .

He forced himself to brush the grains of sand from Leon's cheek. He felt the warmth and pliability of life. He saw the faint stir of breath in Leon's chest. He hesitated, then fumbled to open Leon's shirt. Beneath the bandage, the wound was ugly and purplish-black, but it wasn't bleeding.

Noel had little left of his own clothing with which to make a fresh bandage. Certainly he had nothing clean. He ripped a strip off Leon's shirt, soaked it in the sea to clean it, then folded it into a pad that he pressed gently over the wound and bound it in place with a length of rope.

For medical care it was primitive, but it would have to do for now.

Finished, he sat back on his heels to survey his duplicate. A sudden wave of dizziness passed over him. He shut his eyes a moment, then forced them open. It wasn't relief, not even joy. Nothing that simple. He couldn't tell what he felt, not now. Mostly he was numb and disbelieving, yet it seemed Leon looked more and more lifelike with every passing moment. There was more color in his cheeks now than when Noel had first found him. His pulse was stronger too. It was almost as though he drew strength from Noel's proximity.

Noel frowned at his own fancifulness. Next he'd be imagining he could heal with a touch. He'd been too long out in the sun, and it was time he pulled himself together.

Gently he gathered Leon in his arms and carried him down the beach, stopping every few minutes to rest and regarner his strength. By the time he reached the others he was soaked with sweat and trembling with fatigue. The sun was setting gloriously at his back, filling sky and sea with blazing color. The wispy clouds were gilded with yellow, pink, and lavender. The air had cooled off.

Kona had built a small fire hidden from the bay and was roasting flamingo eggs over coals. He had a stack of fruit and a rock for smashing coconuts. Lady Mountleigh had regained consciousness, but she looked wan and tired as though her head still ached. She seemed confused as to where she was and did not recognize Noel.

Depositing Leon, Noel tried to catch his breath. He felt oddly weak and depleted, but Leon looked even better than before.

Noel dropped cross-legged in the sand with a sigh and picked up a mango. "You've been busy, Kona."

The boy smiled shyly. "Kona good?"

"Kona very good!" Noel looked around. "Where's Neddie?"

Kona shrugged and pointed at the bay. "Gone to headland to make signal."

"What?"

Kona started to repeat his answer, but Noel tossed aside his mango without listening. He stood up.

"That damned brat! Is he crazy? He'll bring the pirates back to us."

"He no listen. He want rescue from white bwana father."

"Damn."

Fuming, Noel headed toward the bay. In the twilight the jungle stood dark and furtive, filled with haunting bird cries and mysterious sounds. And bats, Noel thought warily. His bites were itching now.

The nineteenth and twentieth centuries had been filled with folklore of monsters, vampires, werewolves, and such. People back then liked to scare themselves, probably as a result of the upheavals and changes wrought by the Industrial Revolution and rapid-fire development of technology. Noel didn't think the vampire bats were calling his name right now, but he didn't like venturing out into the shadows and wanted to be back to the campfire before full dark.

On the other hand, his cloud of fatigue was clearing rapidly, so rapidly in fact he suspected Leon *had* been drawing energy from him.

My brother, the vampire, he thought and swallowed the semihysterical desire to laugh.

It was too bad none of the brandy and rum kegs had washed ashore. He could use a stiff drink right now.

He found Neddie on a low promontory, a tiny figure staring out to sea with all his hopes in his face. The boy had removed his ruffled shirt and it fluttered from a tall pole that he'd erected. The hole he'd dug was too shallow to support the height of the pole. It was canted over at an angle. Neddie had tried to correct the problem by bracing the base with rocks and seashells. Naturally that solution hadn't worked. With luck the thing would fall over during the night.

"Neddie," said Noel quietly so he wouldn't startle the boy.

Neddie jumped and whirled around with his hand clutching the stick he carried swordlike through his belt. Noel noticed that he'd whittled a sharp point on the end of it. He also held a razor-sharp clam shell in his hand.

"Time to go back to camp," said Noel. Now that he was here, he wasn't sure he wanted to admonish the child. Neddie was trying hard to cope with the situation, after all. He'd been through a lot in the last couple of days.

"I'm going to keep watch for rescue," said Neddie. "My father will send the Royal Navy in search of us."

"I don't think it's a good idea to be waving a flag."

"Why not?" said Neddie in his aristocratic drawl. He looked down his thin nose in a way that irritated Noel. "One would think you don't want to be rescued. Are you afraid they'll hang you for piracy?"

"I'm not a pirate," said Noel. Then, because he didn't want to go on defending himself, he started to knock down the pole.

Neddie sprang at him. "Don't! Don't!" he cried tearfully. "It's the only way they'll find us."

He wrapped his arms around Noel's waist and tried to block him bodily. Noel stopped and freed himself from Neddie's clutch. Neddie was crying now, his small frame shaking with sobs. Tears streaked down his dirty face.

"I want to go home," he said. "I want to go home."

"You're going to get home," said Noel. "I promise."

"Then why won't you let us be rescued?"

Noel met those baffled, angry eyes. "I want you to be rescued, kid. I'm just afraid Lonigan's pirates will see your flag and come back. We need to keep watch up here instead. If we see a friendly sail, then we can raise the flag. How's that?"

Neddie sniffed and made no answer. Noel took his hand and squeezed it reassuringly.

"Hey," he said. "We don't want the pirates to come back and bother us again, do we?"

Neddie shook his head.

"No. So let's take down the flag. It's a very good one, by the way. We'll leave it here for when we need it."

Noel lowered the pole to the ground.

Neddie watched him, rubbing his eyes and trying to swallow his tears.

"Who's going to keep watch?" he asked.

"We'll take turns," said Noel. "First thing in the morning one of us will—"

"That might be too late!"

"They can't see the flag at night, son," said Noel. "We'll be up here at dawn. All right?"

Reluctantly Neddie gave him a nod. He twisted free of Noel's grip and went back to the camp ahead of Noel. His small back was stiff with resentment. Noel let him be. As long as the boy was quiet with his sulking, Noel didn't care what he did.

At the camp, they found Leon awake and sitting propped up against a broken sea chest that Kona had dragged there for the purpose. In the ruddy light of the campfire, Leon's eyes glittered watchfully. He looked tired and was obviously in pain, but he was better.

Noel dropped down beside him in the sand, making sure he stayed out of reach. He'd given Leon enough energy. He had to make sure Leon didn't drain him to the danger point. Which made the idea of sleeping near each other not such a good idea. He wouldn't put it past Leon to hold his hand all night and drain him dry.

"You're better," said Noel.

Leon dragged up one side of his mouth into a smile. "Hard to kill." His voice was weak, but still full of the old bitter resentment.

Noel frowned, squirming a bit, but it had to be said. "You saved my life last night. Thanks."

Leon made a raspy noise in his throat. After a few seconds Noel realized it was a chuckle. "Does it hurt so much to owe me a favor, brother?"

Noel scowled and busied himself with the flamingo egg that Kona gave him. He broke it open and blew on the soft, cooked insides to cool them.

"Grown shy, brother?" mocked Leon.

"Don't tire yourself," snapped Noel.

"Aren't you going to ask why?"

"No."

"Don't you care?"

Noel threw him a resentful glance. "I care."

Leon's smile broadened. "I thought you would. Now you're in my debt."

Noel spooned himself some egg. "Nope."

"Yes."

"Wrong," said Noel shortly. "You stepped in front of that knife because you can't afford to let me die. You acted from fear and self-preservation, not from altruism."

"The result is the same."

"Sure, but I don't owe you squat."

Leon glared at him, looking baffled now and increasingly angry. "Hypocrite! You're always preaching conscience and principal, but when it comes time to practice them you have a convenient excuse."

"You can't force someone to feel gratitude," said Noel.

"But—"

"If you try," said Noel, interrupting, "you create resentment and sometimes even hatred."

Leon shifted his head fretfully. "You already hate me."

Noel stared a long time at his food. "Not hate," he said at last. "Perhaps . . . pity."

"Pity, hell!" flashed Leon. "As usual you won't admit anything base in yourself. You think I am the only one who has flaws. But you are wrong, Noel, *wrong*! Don't deny that you wish I didn't exist. Don't deny that when we traveled here, you were trying to kill me. You'd kill me now, in cold blood, if you could find a reason to justify it."

He paused, gasping for breath and suddenly white about the mouth. His rain-colored eyes gleamed feverishly, so bitter Noel could not meet them.

Noel's own temper chafed under the tight control he held on it. Leon, as usual, was twisting everything to fit his own bizarre perceptions. And, as usual, they could not spend even five minutes together without picking a quarrel. But Noel wasn't going to explain the black anger that had swept him when Leon manipulated Cody Trask's death. Leon had been put together with something essential missing, and Noel could never make him understand. The fact that Leon himself knew he wasn't complete only drove him to worse behavior.

Glancing up, Noel saw the others watching him and Leon from across the flickering campfire. He could not read their faces. Their expressions were neutral, wary, the way people look when a family argues in public.

"You'd better rest awhile," said Noel, keeping his voice as mild as he could. "Do you want some egg?"

"Go to hell," whispered Leon.

"Are you thirsty?"

Leon hesitated, stubbornness radiating from him. At last, however, he nodded.

"No water, bwana," said Kona to Noel. "No find."

Noel swore to himself. He'd forgotten all about the responsibility of foraging. "There's a freshwater spring that way, in the jungle."

Kona brightened. "We go get?"

"No, not now," said Noel more sharply than he intended. "It's too late."

"Can find, even in dark."

"*No,*" said Noel. "It's not safe. We stick together and we stay by the fire."

Leon made his little rasping chuckle. "Afraid of the dark now, brother?"

Kona, however, looked at Noel with respect tinged with a little apprehension. "Dark gods walk this island, bwana?"

Noel nodded. He walked over to the pile of coconuts and broke one with a rock. Then he handed a half to Leon, who took it with a frown. "Have some coconut milk instead."

Leon stared at it.

"Go on," said Noel. "It's tasty enough."

Leon flung it at him, sending the white milk splattering. "Go to hell! You—"

His voice and strength gave out on him. Gasping, he slumped back with his eyes closed. Noel stared at him a moment, then broke another coconut and knelt beside Leon. He lifted Leon's head and tipped the coconut shell to his lips.

Leon drank some of it, choking a little, then sighed and opened his eyes.

"Don't talk," said Noel. "You're too tired."

Leon's eyes held his. "You know I can't taste food," he muttered. "You know I have to depend on you . . . even for that."

"Yeah," said Noel, feeling pity come back. "I forgot. I wasn't trying to tease you. Go to sleep."

Kona took first watch. Scooping sand to fit his body's contours more comfortably, Noel settled down by the fire close enough to let its smoke drift over him. The scents of ash and flame were comforting. In minutes the rhythmic splash of waves upon the shore lulled him into the deep oblivion of exhaustion.

It seemed he had hardly closed his eyes before Kona was shaking his shoulder. Noel lifted his head, seeing the sleeping forms and dying red embers of the fire without comprehension.

"What's wrong?" he mumbled.

"No wrong, bwana," whispered Kona. "Time for watching."

"Oh." Noel forced himself to sit up and rubbed his face in an effort to wake up. He walked around and inhaled deeply of the balmy air. The sea looked black and flat beyond the tiny cove. Overhead a thin sliver of moon cast no light.

Yawning, Noel settled down near the fire and fed it back to life with small bits of driftwood. The crackling flames were mesmerizing. He watched them flicker hungrily, yellow at the edges, white in the center. The embers hissed and popped.

He yawned again and shook his head as drowsiness crept over him. He reached out to poke the fire again, but his hand felt heavy. It sank to the sand, and the charred stick rolled from his slack fingers.

Pretty flames, he thought vaguely. Their shifting patterns cast black shadows on the ground that writhed and tangled.

Snakes, he thought. *Snakes around us.*

The hissing embers grew louder. The heat intensified until he was sweating. He leaned closer to the fire, fascinated, and the singing flames seemed to be calling him. If he got close enough perhaps he could make out the words. . . .

"Noel!"

His own voice called him. Noel did not listen.

"Noel!"

Terror. Urgency. Noel blinked.

"*Noel!* For God's sake, help me!"

Leon's voice. Leon calling him. Calling him . . .

"Noel! Help me! Please!"

Noel blinked and came aware just in time to avoid toppling into the flames. Scorched, he threw himself back.

"Noel."

It was a mere whisper, fading, fearful. Noel looked over at Leon and saw his duplicate sweating, his lips drawn back in a grimace. Concerned, Noel scrambled over to him and reached for his hand.

"Don't . . . touch me!" said Leon, jerking back from him. "Help me."

He was trembling violently. His back arched in a spasm. Not understanding what was happening, Noel gripped his arms, but Leon cried out and flung him back.

"Stay away," he gasped, obviously struggling to get the words out. His eyes rolled back in his head. "Mondoun . . . wants me." He cried out, a terrible choking, strangled noise. The shudders racking him grew worse.

Noel hesitated a moment, then raised his left wrist. "LOC, activate. Emergency priority access. Activate *now.*"

The LOC remained silent and unresponsive. Noel thumped it fiercely. "Come on, you piece of junk, *activate.*"

Deep, booming laughter from behind him made him spin around. Mondoun's dark face hung suspended in the flames. His laughter rang out loudly, yet the others still slept as though unaware of the danger in their midst. Mondoun's filed teeth reflected the ruddy light of the flames. His tongue looked snake-black.

Snakes, thought Noel, then shook himself.

"Fight him, Leon," he urged. "Don't let him get to you. Count backward. Count in Greek backward."

Leon writhed, moaning. "Can't," he gasped. "Baba . . ."

"Don't call to him. Don't listen to him," said Noel.

But even as he spoke he knew that Leon wasn't strong enough. The dark side of Leon would always surrender. Already Leon's struggles were lessening. Leon's eyes glazed over, and some of the terror faded from his face.

Noel did not let himself hesitate. Seizing a chunk of drift-wood, he thrust it into the fire until it caught. Then holding it aloft as a torch, he hurried up the beach and followed the jungle trail to the hillside spring and beyond to the cave where Mondoun worked his black magic.

A wind blew up from nowhere, gusting strongly. The torch nearly went out. Noel shielded it as best he could and kept going. Roots made him stumble.

He squinted ahead in the faint light at the overgrown trail. Overhead the tree limbs seemed to reach down for him, snagging his clothing, poking at his eyes. Things chattered and gibbered from the branches.

"Go back," breathed the wind.

"Go back," rustled the trees.

"Go back," crackled the torch flames.

In the distance a bird shrieked, and Noel nearly jumped from his skin. He stumbled to a momentary halt and wiped the sweat from his face. His heart was thudding double time. His lungs felt as though they had a knot tied in them. Goose bumps were standing up on his arms and his blood felt like ice water. Yet he was hot as though he stood near a bonfire.

Then, they came.

He'd been dreading them since he left the dubious safety of the campfire. When he heard the faint squeaking and twittering and the leathery rustle of wings beating the air, his heart bolted into his mouth and he nearly cringed to the ground in fear.

It was a trap. It had to be. The attack on Leon occurred to lure him up the hillside, and he'd fallen for the whole thing just as Baba Mondoun had intended him to.

Noel squinted at the night sky, but the torchlight affected his night vision and he couldn't see the bats. He could hear them, though. One swooped at his head. He ducked, then swore and swung the torch at it.

Squeaking, it flashed away. Others dived at him, and he held them off with the torch too, sweating, his heart quaking. If even one of them lit on him and sank in its fangs, he knew he'd give way to the unreasoning terror building inside him. To hold it at bay, he shouted at them, cursed them, hooted at them.

When they drew back, he fought the urge to retreat. Trap or not, he had to confront Mondoun once and for all, now that he definitely knew the man was here. Anything was better than creeping around the island in perpetual uneasiness, waiting for the man to strike.

The bats attacked again. One landed between his shoulder blades. Panicking, Noel ran backward and smashed the creature against a tree. He heard the tiny bones crack and the thing fell to the ground.

"Get away from me, damn you!" he shouted and ran.

They dived at his head, but with less aggression than before. Then he was scrambling up the escarpment to the cave mouth.

The bats vanished as suddenly as they had appeared. Even the breeze died down. All grew still and silent. Noel couldn't even hear the insects singing in the undergrowth now.

The cave mouth lay in darkness. No light shone from it. As he approached cautiously, Noel felt as though it contained an element blacker even than night.

Don't spook yourself more you already are, he told himself. *Stop imagining things.*

As he stepped inside the air temperature dropped from balmy tropic to bitter cold. He shivered and went on.

Five steps into the cave, the torch abruptly went out.

Total darkness surrounded him with such immediacy it was like being swallowed. His wits plunged, and he was frozen, unable to move, unable to decide what he should do next.

All he had to do was back straight out. He didn't have to tackle the *Bocor*. If Leon degenerated a little more, it hardly mattered. Noel could live on one end of the island and Mondoun could have the other. As a truce, that was simple enough to arrange.

Sure it was.

He knew Mondoun would never leave them alone. And if Noel didn't find some way to salvage Leon from the *Bocor*'s clutches, then he would feel guilty for having failed his duplicate, and perhaps himself.

His breath was coming so short and fast that he feared he would hyperventilate. But he forced himself to get a grip.

"Baba Mondoun!" he called.

His voice echoed through the passageway and into the cave beyond. Noel's mouth had dried up. He swallowed.

"Hey, Mondoun!" he called with all the insolence he could muster. "If you wanted to talk to me, all you had to do was yell. No need for this mumbo-jumbo business with the campfire. I admit it was impressive, but don't you get tired after using all that energy?"

Mondoun said nothing. But an orange glow spread through the passageway, brightening as it came. It sucked the darkness away, and when it reached Noel's bare feet he could not help jumping aside.

Yet it was only light, and he felt somewhat foolish at being afraid of it.

He could see the rough-hewn walls of limestone now. The sandy ground curved around a bend in the passageway.

The stick in his hand with its charred end white with ash offered little comfort. As a weapon it was less than useless. But it was all he had.

Noel swallowed hard again, and walked forward.

He had to duck his head to enter the small cavern. He did so reluctantly, expecting an attack of some kind.

Nothing happened. The place looked deserted.

Let down, Noel frowned and gazed around. The torches set in crude iron wall sconces were unlit. The fire pit held no flames. There was no visible source of the strange orange light, soft and diffuse, yet it provided clear illumination. On the scuffed ground lay a bunch of dried herbs, tied with a grisly amulet made from bits of animal skin and bone. Baba's hat and wig were there too, tossed down as though abandoned.

The cave stank of blood, herbs, and smoke. Beneath those mingled odors ran a fetid stench of decay and rot that made Noel's nostrils wrinkle.

"Mondoun!" he said loudly.

His voice echoed around him, mocking him, then at last it faded.

In the silence, Noel heard the scrape of a footstep behind him. He whirled, his heart thudding fast, but it was only the wind rustling through the passageway.

He frowned in growing puzzlement. Wind? Wind couldn't reach this deep into the cave.

A screech as shrill as fingernails on a chalkboard sounded from above him. Startled, Noel barely had time to look up at the shadowy stone ceiling before two figures detached themselves from it and dropped onto him.

Panic flared white in his mind. *Huge bats,* he thought, even as their weight bore him down. His head thudded on the ground, and he grimaced in a sick twist of pain. They were swarming across him, almost as big as he, hot and sweaty and . . . human.

Realization blinked on in his brain, and he stopped his frantic struggling. They flipped him onto his back and held his arms pinned so he couldn't rise.

Noel stared. The two men were black and obviously some of the slaves he had freed from the hold of the *Plentitude* last night. Completely naked except for the amulets swinging around their necks, they held him helpless with an attitude of indifference. Their eyes were glazed and blank. Their faces had a slackness that gave him the creeps.

"Hey!" he said angrily, trying to get their attention. *"Hey!"* They ignored him.

Noel struggled to twist loose. He curled up his feet and kicked the one on his left, knocking him aside. The other one was slow to react, and Noel yanked free. Scrambling around, he climbed to his feet to run, but Baba Mondoun's sudden appearance from the passageway brought him up short.

Panting, he stared at the *Bocor.*

Mondoun's lips pulled back from his filed teeth. They were stained red with fresh blood. His booming laughter echoed through the cave and made goose bumps rise on Noel's skin.

"Cut the fun and games," snapped Noel. "We're all shipwrecked on this sandbar together. We have to think about survival, not—"

"The hour of the gods has come," said Mondoun. He lifted his hands and gazed at the ceiling. "They are here," he said reverently.

The LOC grew warm on Noel's wrist. Startled, for he'd thought it completely inactive, Noel touched it.

"There are many forms of power," said Mondoun. "Not all are such as you command, *Hongoun.*"

"I don't—"

"You command the future. You have kept me from it. But I have another servant now."

As he spoke, Mondoun stepped aside. Leon stood behind him, a pale, glassy-eyed Leon who entered like a sleepwalker.

Noel's heart sank. He stared, disbelieving. "You made a zombie of him."

Mondoun's smirk widened.

"But he's able to protect himself. He has abilities—telepathy and—"

"Always you seek explanations from the land of what seems rather than from the land of what *is,*" said Mondoun. His resonant voice dropped to a near whisper. His eyes gleamed fanatically. "Look at the shadows, *Hongoun,* and believe."

"No!"

Despite himself, Noel took a step back. He was conscious of the two zombies at his back, however. The cave was getting hotter, uncomfortably so, although there was no visible source of heat. Sweat beaded on Noel's forehead.

Mondoun reached out and sketched a pattern in the air with his fingertip. Noel could not stop himself from watching, half expecting to see smoke hover there, yet he saw nothing.

He struggled to keep his wits, to not let himself become trapped by another of Mondoun's spells. "What do you want from us? What do you want with *him?*"

Mondoun swung his head back and forth, slowly, rhythmically, like a cobra head swaying before its intended victim. "He is but your shadow. To possess him is to command a wraith. You, however, have the power of the future. I would have that power."

"It doesn't work," said Noel. "The LOC is damaged."

"You lie."

"I don't. See for yourself—"

"Noel."

The whisper seemed to come from nowhere. It made Noel start and forget what he was saying. He glanced at Leon, who still stared at nothing. Yet it was Leon who had spoken his name in a desperate plea.

A grimace crossed Mondoun's face. For a moment he looked uncertain, even fatigued. Then he scowled furiously and barked a command that Noel's translator did not recognize.

Leon didn't blink, didn't move, but he turned paler. Watching him, Noel felt a surge of unwanted compassion. If Mondoun wasn't stopped, they'd both be zombies, held prisoner with hypnotism and some kind of awful concoction made from toad poison and God knew what else. No, thanks.

"Forget it, Mondoun," he said crisply. "No deal. I don't have any power to share with you, and I wouldn't even if the thing worked."

"Noel."

"Silence!" roared Mondoun. He turned on Leon and struck him, but his hand passed right through Leon's chest as though Leon was only a hologram.

Even Noel blinked, confounded. Then he realized what was happening and stepped forward in alarm.

"Release him," he said urgently. "Mondoun, let him go *now.*"

"He is mine," said Mondoun.

"You don't understand. He's disappearing, ceasing to exist in this dimension." Leon had once before been sucked into the time vortex, with disastrous results. Noel wasn't going to let that happen again. "You've got to let him go. If he passes through, we're—"

"Do not command me!" shouted Mondoun. "Ignorant one, do you not yet know with what you deal?"

"Let him go!" shouted Noel back. "Leon, fight it. Fight to stay here. If you reenter the time vortex, you'll—"

"Cease!" said Mondoun. "He is mine. He listens to me."

"He's vanishing," said Noel savagely. "Once he disappears completely, that's it. He won't come back."

Mondoun cocked his head and regarded Noel for a long moment. Leon by now was so transparent Noel could see through him. His fingers had vanished completely. The mist of nothingness crept up his legs.

Desperate and frustrated, Noel rammed his fingers through his hair. "What will make you listen?"

"You," said Mondoun.

Noel blinked. "What? I don't understand."

"Come to me of your own free will. Surrender to me, Noel Kedran. Cease to fight me, and I shall have no need of your shadow."

Noel recoiled. Sacrifice himself for Leon? That scuzzy, unprincipled, sociopathic good-for-nothing duplication who was unwanted and unneeded, who had done nothing but cause trouble since he came into existence?

Noel, help me.

Leon's cry was only in his mind now. Noel heard it clearly, however, and was astonished. For the first time they communicated mentally, and Leon's fear traveled straight into him.

I don't want to die.

I'm sorry. I can't help you, replied Noel.

I need you, brother.

I'm not your brother!

Help me. Don't leave me out here between the time streams.

I can't help you.

I'm afraid!

Leon had nearly dissolved now. Only a vague outline of his body remained. His eyes held naked despair.

Noel could not bear it. Yet he could not do what Mondoun asked, either. He could never do it.

"Come to me," whispered Mondoun. "Join the *Congo* and the dark—"

"No!" shouted Noel.

He launched himself bodily, tackling Mondoun and bringing him down. Mondoun had a longer reach and despite the disadvantage of having been taken by surprise, he squirmed sinuously free of Noel's grasp and thrust Noel off.

Noel hit the wall with a grunt and threw himself at Mondoun again. The *Bocor* fended him off, but the physical struggle obviously distracted him. Leon flickered back into view, and the two Africans called out bewildered questions in their own tongue.

Mondoun snarled a word that took physical shape and hovered, burning with tiny flames, in the air.

Noel scooped up a handful of dirt and flung it at the word. The flames extinguished, and the word vanished. Dismay crossed Mondoun's face. Noel drove a punch deep into his stomach, and the black man doubled over, wheezing.

Leon popped back into existence, and crumpled to the ground. One of the Africans screamed, then the orange light vanished, and they were plunged into darkness.

Noel grabbed desperately at Mondoun, but the man twisted in his grasp, hissing like a python. Noel found himself slammed back against the wall so hard the breath was knocked from him, and Mondoun jerked free.

"You will regret," said Mondoun's voice, sounding exhausted and furious. "You will see Baba's revenge. I will call the pirates back to this island, and they will roast your tongues from your skulls. They will nail your feet to planks and hang you upside down until you scream for mercy. They will—"

Noel followed his voice and pounced blindly. He connected, and Mondoun cried out as Noel shoved him into the wall.

"Take him to the spring and drown him," said Leon, still gasping for breath.

Mondoun sprang free and although Noel did his best to follow the man through the passageway, he blundered in the darkness and could not retake the *Bocor*. By the time Noel burst, panting and sweat-soaked, outside into the cool air, there was no evidence of where Mondoun had vanished to. The jungle rustled and twittered with purposes of its own. Noel listened but heard no crashing progress through the undergrowth. Mondoun could be long gone by now, heading for another hiding place on the island, or he could be lurking nearby, waiting for the chance to attack again.

Noel felt suddenly uneasy. "Leon, come on," he called in a low voice. "Get out here. Let's return to camp."

Leon took so long to appear, Noel was ready to abandon him. When he did finally emerge from the passageway, he was carrying the herb bundle with the amulet tied around it.

Exasperated, Noel snatched it from him and threw it away. "Leave that stuff alone!"

"It was just some weeds," began Leon defensively. "Smelled better than whatever used to live in there."

"Never mind," said Noel shortly. He could not shake off the worry that Mondoun had other tricks lying in wait for them. "Let's get back to our camp."

"Not so fast," said Leon, wheezing. He leaned against a tree. "Let me catch my breath."

"Will you come on?" said Noel impatiently. "The sooner we're back, the sooner—"

"Sure," retorted Leon. "And what's so safe about the camp? He reached us there. He can reach us anywhere. And why didn't you use the LOC to break his concentration? That electromagnetic field would be strong enough, if projected externally, to—"

"The LOC doesn't work," said Noel.

He listened to Leon's silence and felt the unspoken reproach. Noel's throat felt choked, his eyes hot. He'd been avoiding thinking about the implications, but if he went on explaining, then the facts had to be faced.

Leon cleared his throat. "You said it was damaged. I thought that was a lie to fool Mondoun."

"No."

"You serious?"

Noel's temper snapped. "Yes, of course I'm serious! You think I'd joke about something as vital as the LOC?"

"Vital for you maybe."

"Oh, right," said Noel. "Don't even start in on your usual whine about how underprivileged you are without a LOC of your own. Just be glad I saved your hide from dissolving in the time vortex."

Leon shoved himself away from the tree and stumbled down the hill in the darkness. "What do you expect from me, groveling?"

"How about a thank you?"

Leon snorted. "After I had to beg like a—"

"I saved you, didn't I?"

"Only because you're afraid I'll block your chances of being recovered if I'm floating around in the time vortex. It seems to me you gave me a lecture not too long ago about not demanding gratitude because it would only turn sour. You're just as self-serving as I am, *brother,* only I admit it and you won't. That's what I can't stand . . . your damned hypocrisy."

Noel frowned. "You're twisting everything again. I—"

"Don't justify it."

"I'm justifying nothing!" Noel caught his arm and jerked him around, wringing a choked cry from Leon. His duplicate swayed, and Noel steadied him, realizing he had yanked on Leon's left arm and probably pulled the wound.

"Sorry," said Noel.

Leon held his left arm clamped against his side. After a moment he drew himself away from Noel's support. "Go to hell," he muttered.

"Why are you always like this?" demanded Noel. "Why can't you try to make a truce? We're here, and we're going to be here for the rest of our lives. The LOC is finished. I can't fix it."

"Have you tried?"

"Yes, I've tried," said Noel angrily. "I've run diagnostic scans until—"

"No, I mean really tried to fix it. As in open the casing."

"With what, a rock and a mallet?" retorted Noel sarcastically.

Leon strode on, weaving now and then, but keeping his back to Noel.

With a sigh, Noel followed him. "We have to find some means of sticking together. Mondoun will have less chance of manipulating us if we—"

"I don't want a truce," said Leon, thrusting aside a branch and letting it whip behind him to smack into Noel. "I don't want to work with you. I don't want to stick together. If Mondoun does call the pirates back, I'm going to rejoin them. After all, I was Lonigan's quartermaster."

"You're hopeless," said Noel in disgust.

Leon stopped and turned to face him. "Wrong. I'm not hopeless. I'm hopeful. Finally I have a real chance to belong. You've robbed me of that everywhere we've traveled. Now I can be free of you."

"Is that what you want?" asked Noel.

The hatred seething from Leon was as strong as ever. His pleas for help, his moments of calm communication with Noel this afternoon, might never have happened. Now that he was out of danger, he had reverted instantly to his spiteful nature.

"Is that really what you want?" asked Noel again.

"Isn't it what you want?" said Leon. "Isn't it always what you want? We traveled here with your hands around my throat, remember?"

"I remember." Noel hesitated. "We can go past that."

"You want me to turn into something as spineless as yourself. Prating of conscience, lacking the ambition to accomplish anything. Bah! I don't want to be like you. Now leave me alone."

"Leon, wait."

"No!" said Leon and walked on. "I'm going to make a bonfire so Lonigan's lookouts will know someone's still alive. If nothing else we can hold the woman and her brat for ransom."

"Leon—"

"Go to hell, Noel! You can't stop me, not anymore. You don't have the LOC to tell you the future and give you an advantage over me. You're on your own now."

"But—"

"For the sake of old times, I'll give you a warning. Hide now while you have the chance. If the pirates catch you again, you won't have a prayer."

"Are you sure you want that to happen?" asked Noel.

Leon threw back his head and laughed. "You still don't understand, do you?"

"Understand what?"

"You can't feel it, can you?"

"Feel what?"

Leon laughed again, laughed until Noel feared he would bring Mondoun down upon them.

"Shut up," said Noel, glancing over his shoulder. "What's gotten into you?"

"Didn't you hear me when I spoke to you from the vortex?"

"Yes, I heard. Why do you think I rescued you?"

"We've never linked directly before. Never. I've tried and tried to touch your mind, but I couldn't."

Noel frowned uneasily, made wary by the glee in Leon's voice. "Good. I don't want to be manipulated by you."

"Stupid! Do I have to spell everything out for you?"

Noel thought it through. "You're saying the LOC protected me?"

"I don't know. I don't care. I'm free. I feel this pain. I can stick my tongue to the bark of this tree and taste it. I'm not a shadow anymore. I'm *real*."

Noel drew in his breath sharply, trying to comprehend what Leon was saying. "You mean—"

"That's right, brother. I'm just as real as you, now. I have just as much right to be here as you. Whatever dominance you had once as the original is gone. There is no more original and copy. There are only two of us. Equal."

"No," said Noel involuntarily.

"Yes! I tell you, yes! Now hide yourself. It's the last favor I'll ever give you. I mean that."

He glared at Noel a moment longer, then turned and walked on through the darkness.

CHAPTER 11

Shortly before noon the next day, Neddie—ever vigilant for rescue—spotted sails and came scooting down the trunk of a palm tree with a whoop of excitement.

"It's the Navy! They've come, Mama! They've come!"

Running and waving his arms, Neddie skirted the construction site, where Noel and Kona labored to build a shelter more substantial than the palm frond lean-to shading Lady Mountleigh. Using timber felled by the storm and boards salvaged from the wreckage, they hoped to erect a small cabin that would at least keep out the daily rain showers. Neddie had scorned this project, declaring that they wouldn't be here long enough to need a cabin, and refused to help.

Now he dashed by heedlessly, kicking up sand as he went.

"Come on! Come on!" he shouted. "They're here."

Noel made an effort to slow him down, but the boy skipped past his fingers.

"You can't catch me," taunted Neddie and stuck out his tongue at Noel. "I knew the Navy would come. Mama, did you hear? The Navy—"

Noel turned and gazed worriedly out to sea. Kona dropped the stick he'd been using to tamp dirt around the base of a corner post and began backing quietly away.

"Wait, Kona," said Noel.

"It's the Navy, the Navy!" chanted Neddie, scampering about in his own version of a hornpipe. "They'll make Kona a slave again. And they'll hang you."

Noel did his best to ignore the child. Lady Mountleigh, languishing in her nest of palm fronds, nibbled wanly on mangoes and made no attempt to chastise her offspring.

"No slave again," said Kona fiercely, still backing away. "No slave!"

Noel stared at the ship but it was still too far away to see clearly. Shading his eyes, he squinted and longed for a spyglass. The ship hovered on the expanse of blue water. It was either moving slowly or it was just hanging out there.

After a sleepless night, Noel wasn't eager for it to be either Lonigan's crew of cutthroats or the Royal Navy. If he had to be exiled here, then he wanted to be left alone.

"We can hide in the caves," he said slowly. He gazed around at the marked-off square and the stack of boards they'd assembled. "We'll have to brush out our tracks and conceal some of this. We'd better get started."

"You tell," said Kona. "I do."

"You can't hide," said Neddie. "I shall tell them where you are, and they will drag you forth and put you in chains."

Kona turned on him. "And maybe young heart go to the *Bocor* after all."

Neddie turned pale. "Mama!"

Lady Mountleigh sat up. "Really, Mr. Kedran, can't you keep this man of yours under control? I won't have my son threatened by a savage."

Noel barely bit back a scathing retort. The woman was too indulgent of her little spoiled brat, but she wasn't well either. He wasn't going to yell at an injured woman.

"Look," he began as they all glared at him. "We can deal with personnel management problems later. Right now I think we need to be very careful, and not assume it's rescue just because of your hopes."

Neddie frowned at him, then spun around and ran past Noel without a word.

"Oh, dear," said Lady Mountleigh. "You've set off his temper. He'll be in the sulks now for hours. It's not good for him to be rushing about so much in this heat. I do wish you wouldn't distress him so, Mr. Kedran. He's highly strung."

"He's a spoiled brat," said Noel.

Lady Mountleigh flushed. She lifted her plump chin. "Your criticism is not appreciated, Mr. Kedran. You may have assumed leadership of our group, but with rescue at hand I think you should consider yourself no longer in charge. Kindly refrain from future offerings of your unsolicited opinion in regards to my son and myself."

Noel stared at her in disbelief. What on earth did she think she was doing playing the grande dame now and putting on airs? If she had any sense at all, she should know better.

"Fine," he snapped. "If you don't want my help, I'll get out of your way. But you might consider the wisdom of caution, lady. If those are pirates instead of the Navy—"

"Nonsense!"

"The rumor going around is that Lonigan has his treasure buried here. Whether that's true or not doesn't matter much at the moment. What does matter is that ship may not be friendly."

She raised her plump hands to her mouth and began to tremble. "I do not like your tone. I have never been spoken to so sharply by a servant, and I will not brook such insolence—"

"I've had enough of this," said Noel. He threw up his hands and started toward her. "You're going to hide in the caves until we know if that's a friendly ship out there. No more arguing, because I'll drag you up the hill by your hair if I have to."

She shrank from him, terror-stricken and foolish. "Please, oh, please! I beg you—"

"Bwana," said Kona worriedly.

Noel shot Lady Mountleigh a look of complete disgust. She was half swooning and sobbing with rapid little hiccups. Pamela Davenport would have already been halfway to the caves, fully aware of the potential danger of this situation and capable of coping with it.

"Bwana!"

Noel turned around. "Yes, what is it?"

Kona pointed at the curve of the bay. Squinting, Noel saw Neddie picking his way through the scrub and rocks up the slope of the promontory. Gulls scattered ahead of him. Their shrieks failed to disturb the flock of flamingoes on the shore. Bright pink birds slept with their heads tucked under their wings, guarded by a lone sentinel balanced on one thin leg. The palms swayed gently. The waves rolled in and slobbered over white sand. Out to sea, the ship seemed to have turned aside as though it meant to pass them by. But if Neddie waved his flag and caught the lookout's attention, they would come to investigate.

Grim irritation settled over Noel. He and Kona looked at each other.

"He's going to wave that damned white flag," said Noel.

Kona cocked his head to one side. "I stop?"

"No, you help Lady Mountleigh to the caves. I'll stop him."

Striding fast, Noel crossed the beach, startling the flamingoes that flew over the water. He headed up the slope to the top of the headland, wincing as the weeds scratched his bare feet and the rocks bruised his toes.

"Neddie!" he called. "Dammit, come back here!"

He lost sight of the boy while he climbed the last few feet. But when he stood on top, sure enough, Neddie had his flagpole erected again, and was securing its balance with a stack of hand-sized rocks and shells. The white shirt tied to the pole flapped halfheartedly, then swelled out in the breeze.

"Dammit!" said Noel. "Take that down."

Neddie gave a little cry and worked faster to secure the pole. "They're leaving," he said desperately. "They're sailing on by."

"Can you see their flag?" asked Noel.

"It's the Union Jack."

Noel stared across the distance himself and saw the brilliant flash of red, white, and blue that represented England. For a brief moment he was disconcerted. It seemed he'd been overreacting, but after Leon's and Mondoun's threats last night caution seemed the best policy.

Another flag fluttered beneath the Union Jack, however. The ship turned gracefully, her white sails billowing and stately. The second flag streamed out plainly, and Noel saw it was black with white crossbones on it.

He drew in his breath sharply, and felt ice water in his veins. "Look, Neddie," he said in a voice raw with dismay. "Look what they're flying."

Neddie's blue eyes widened. He stared, his small body frozen.

"What is it, Neddie?"

Neddie's mouth trembled. "The—the Jolly Roger."

Noel ran his hands through his hair with disgust and turned around to jerk down the flag. Neddie crouched behind some rocks, but Noel saw no need now to hide. Anyone with a spyglass could see him clearly. Nevertheless, he crouched beside Neddie and watched, holding his breath in hope that the lookout would think it was only a reflection of the sun on the waves that he'd seen, and not a signal for help.

Yet the ship came on, close enough now for her flat deck and high gunwales to show. Her prow rose and dipped steadily. Men clung like monkeys in her rigging.

Noel told himself not to panic. He could figure out a plan of defense. There had to be a way to keep himself and the others free from Lonigan's crew.

How? asked a despairing corner of his mind.

Without weapons, all they could do was hide. And Noel figured Mondoun knew every inch of the caves honeycombing the island's squat hill. The *Bocor* would lead the pirates right to them.

"I'm afraid," whispered Neddie.

Noel put his hand briefly on the boy's small shoulder. "Me too."

"How touching," said Leon's mocking voice.

Startled, Noel whirled around and found himself gazing into Leon's pale silver eyes. Leon stood there in his tattered, salt-stained clothing. His left arm had been tucked up in a makeshift sling. His free hand held a dagger. He looked a bit drawn about the mouth, but there was a glow in him, a fierce exultation that Noel didn't trust.

"Where did you get the knife?" asked Noel. "From Mondoun?"

Leon grinned. "You might say I found it."

Noel frowned. "What happens now? What about Lady Mountleigh and the boy?"

Leon shrugged his good shoulder. "That's up to Lonigan."

"It doesn't have to be. Let them go. Let them hide. Tell Lonigan they drowned."

"Why should I?" said Leon with an incredulous laugh.

"They aren't a part of this—"

"Seems to me they are." Leon bent over slightly and stared at Neddie. The boy shrank nearer to Noel, and Leon smiled a cruel, malevolent smile. "What's the matter, brother, are you afraid I'll change history again? You're a fool! You always were. You're trapped here the same as me. Why should you care what we do or what we tamper with?"

"I care," said Noel thickly.

Leon snorted.

"Leon, please. Let them hide in the caves—"

"Caves?" Leon started laughing. "Noel, my stupid brother, you never stop amazing me. Lonigan's treasure is in the caves."

At first Noel didn't understand. He stared at Leon's grinning face and frowned. "What?"

"His treasure! Chests of it. Doubloons, pieces of eight, Dutch silver, and jewels! Rubies, emeralds, strings of enormous pearls. Spices from the Orient. Kegs of rum. Gunpowder. Bolts of silks and velvets. I found it, and now it's mine."

As he spoke, he swaggered closer to Noel and pulled a handful of gold coins from his pocket. He tossed them carelessly at Noel's feet. Neddie bent to pick them up, but Noel gripped his shoulder.

"Leave them," he said quietly, his eyes never leaving Leon's face.

"But—"

Noel's gaze shifted briefly to Neddie. "Blood was shed to acquire that money."

"Oh, poppycock!" said Leon with scorn. "Why fill the brat's head with that kind of romantic mush? Money is money. It has no morals of its own. It can't be tainted. It belongs to whoever is smart enough to acquire it and keep it." Leon threw back his head with another shout of laughter. "Lonigan acquired it, but I'm going to keep it."

"Are you crazy?" said Noel. "He'll draw and quarter you."

"Not if he can't find it," said Leon, chuckling. "Not if we hide it and don't tell him where it is. There's no time to lose, brother. We've got to move it before he comes ashore."

It was risky, but Noel saw that it was the only chance they had. Still, he looked at Leon with suspicion. "Last night you were threatening me for eternity. You said you intended to stick with Lonigan and be a pirate for—"

"And now I've changed my tune?" broke in Leon.

"Yeah."

"My motives are simple. I change with the wind. Whatever opportunity presents itself, I follow it. But to do this, I need your help. Don't be stupid, Noel. Without my plan you're lost."

Noel looked away, but he knew Leon was right. He also knew that Leon wouldn't have approached him with this offer if he could have shifted the treasure alone. As soon as Leon no longer needed Noel's help, he would betray Noel.

"Hey, I was a little upset last night. A touch feverish maybe. Mondoun got under my skin. I said things I didn't mean. You don't intend to hold a grudge, do you?"

Leon's wheedling tone was so patently false Noel glared at him. "Don't push it," he said.

Leon smiled. "Then stop wasting time."

He started away, but Noel knelt before Neddie and gripped him hard by the arms. Neddie wore his sulky, distrustful look again. Noel shook him to get his attention.

"I want you to take your mother and Kona and hide in the rocks on the west side of the island, where I found you yesterday. Can you do that? It's up to you to protect them."

Neddie twisted free of Noel's grip. In silence he picked up his flag and stuck the pole back into the ground. His eyes, hot with defiance, met Noel's.

"Okay, leave your flag. It can't hurt us now," said Noel. "Just do what I ask, will you? Don't let the pirates know you're here."

Without a word Neddie scrambled down the slope with the easy agility of childhood.

"Come on!" urged Leon. "They'll be in the cove, dropping anchor in a few minutes."

"I hope the kid follows orders," said Noel worriedly.

"Will you forget that brat and his overweight mama? They're no concern of yours. Now, hurry while there's still time!"

They slithered down the far side of the promontory and plodded through the hot sand to the construction site. Lady Mountleigh's lean-to was gone as though it had never been. The boards were scattered about in an aimless fashion. Sand half covered some of them. All the tracks had been smoothed away.

Noel whistled in admiration. "Kona's been busy."

"Forget Kona," snapped Leon, picking up a frond and using it to wipe out his own tracks. "Keep low. We've got to make those trees before they see us."

It was hard trying to run, crouch, and brush tracks all at the same time. Finally they made the relative safety of the jungle and plunged into the undergrowth.

The humid scent of decay and damp earth filled Noel's nostrils. Uneasy, he could not keep from glancing around. Bats didn't fly during the day, but Mondoun might have some other varieties of helpers. Those two zombies of his, for example.

"What about the *Bocor*?" whispered Noel as he followed Leon through the thicket.

A bird squawked ahead of them, like a herald. Leon didn't bother to glance back. "Don't worry about him."

"I *do* worry about him. He's on Lonigan's side."

"No more than me," said Leon. "Quit worrying. He's probably off in his lair killing chickens."

"There are no chickens on this island," said Noel.

"Maybe he's extracting toad poison then. Forget him."

"I don't think it's a good idea to count him out of anything."

"He's not a factor right now," said Leon impatiently and quickened his pace.

They avoided the trail to the spring and circled around to the north side of the hill, taking a route Noel had not traveled before. No matter how confident Leon was, Noel kept his wits sharp and his eyes on the move. He didn't want to be taken by surprise again. Surprises on this island tended to be nasty.

The jungle thinned out, and Leon started up a narrow trail that looked suitable for goats but little else. Hugging the hillside and trying to keep his balance, Noel doubted they were going to be carrying any treasure chests out this way, but he said nothing.

The cave mouth itself was only a narrow opening, set at an angle and about Noel's height. Leon squeezed through, grunting as though he bumped his wound. After being nearly dead yesterday, he was hopping around today with remarkable energy. Maybe he was a fast healer. Or maybe his seconds in the time vortex had aided his recovery. Noel knew that traveling deleted injuries because of the time lapse. If he got hurt in the fourteenth century, he wasn't injured in the nineteenth. So if he traveled from the fourteenth to the nineteenth, he lost the injury.

"Get in here!" said Leon.

With a blink, Noel pulled himself together and squeezed inside the cave. It smelled cool and musty, but nothing had apparently made a den of it recently, and it lacked the odors of Mondoun's craft. Noel stopped and blinked, trying to let his vision adjust to the darkness.

A slight amount of light came in from the cave mouth. The cave itself was cramped. Leon slipped through a passageway at the rear of it, and Noel followed with increasing reluctance.

He bumped into Leon, who swore at him.

"Sorry," mumbled Noel. "I can't see anything."

"Just be still," said Leon.

He fumbled with something. Noel heard a scrape, then a spark flared. Leon struck another spark from his flint and steel, then threw some bits of dried grass over the embers to encourage a minute flame.

Feebly it ate the grass. Leon broke a stick into bits and fed it carefully until it crackled steadily. Then he tucked his flint and steel into a tinderbox and pocketed it. Taking a pitch-soaked brand from a nearby barrel, he thrust it into the fire until it caught, then held his torch aloft.

"Come and see," he said with a grin.

Around a bend in the passageway they entered a spacious cave, and Noel stopped in his tracks at the sight before him.

Iron-bound sea chests stood stacked in disorder. Some were still locked; others had been flung open. Fabulous gemstones glittered in the torchlight. Noel bent over and picked up a diamond and ruby necklace worth a king's ransom. It sparkled and flashed in his fingers. The center ruby was the size of a small walnut. Noel stared at it, mesmerized.

"Look at this," said Leon.

He flung open a chest to reveal a heap of gold coins. "Pieces of eight. Aren't they magnificent? And since eight is the symbol for infinity it's only fitting that we have these, don't you think?"

Noel picked up one of the coins and turned it over in his fingers.

Another chest held silver. Another held a service of gold plate engraved with a Spanish coat of arms.

Bolts of brilliant silk stood stacked against a wall. Leon toppled them, and streamers of crimson, purple, yellow, and green unrolled across the dusty floor.

"Look at it! It's ours, Noel. It's ours!"

Noel broke himself loose from the spell. Dropping the necklace back with the other jewelry, he shook his head. "Not yet. We can't possibly hide all this. I doubt we can even pick up one of these chests. We'd need a mule and a couple of days to move all of it."

"Use your head," snapped Leon. "Don't you think I know that?"

He gripped Noel's arm. "Come and see."

Noel pulled free, irked as always by Leon's touch. But he followed Leon to the opening on the other side of the cave.

"The passageway from the south forks here. There are multiple caves on this side of the passageway," said Leon excitedly. "We wall up this one, and he'll think the treasure's gone when it really isn't."

Noel stared at him a long moment, then rolled his eyes. "You're kidding."

"No."

"You're kidding."

Leon scowled. "It will work. With stones and mud—"

"This is ludicrous," said Noel. "Are you out of your mind?"

"It will work," insisted Leon angrily.

Noel couldn't believe he'd let himself be dragged along on this wild goose chase. "And where are we going to get stones?"

Leon pointed in silence. After a long moment, Noel reluctantly walked in that direction. He peered into a tiny chamber and saw a vast pile of stones, ranging from the size of his fist to the size of a cannonball. Someone had stacked these into a sort of crude altar.

Figurines daubed with blood and feathers hung from bolts driven into the walls. The place stank.

Noel withdrew quickly. "One of Mondoun's playpens."

"Doesn't matter," said Leon. "Let's get to work."

Reluctantly, Noel started carrying stones out and stacking them in the entry to the treasure cave. This wasn't going to work, not in a million years. He kept telling himself that, but he went on working. He lacked a better plan, and however cockeyed this one was, it was better than nothing.

While he stacked the stones, Leon went off and returned with a pail of mud that he'd mixed somewhere.

"Mondoun must live in here somewhere," said Noel. "If he finds us . . ."

"If Lonigan finds us, then you can worry," said Leon. He started smearing the thick mud while Noel kept building the wall. "I've found more of Mondoun's toys. If the pirates decide to check on their treasure, we'll start off by blowing some of Baba's pretty smoke through the passageways. They'll be so high on that stuff they won't even remember what they're here for."

Fortunately the entry grew narrower as it went up. Noel's wall went fast. But he was still skeptical.

"Then," said Leon happily, "we'll sneak around and take their ship. Once we have control of the deck cannon we can sweep the beach with shot and hold them off. We'll have—"

"Hold it!" said Noel sharply. "Who said anything about taking their ship? We're outnumbered—"

"Can't you do anything but protest? I thought you had guts."

"Yeah, and I'd like to keep them intact," said Noel. "Our purpose here is survival. I'm not helping you rule the high seas."

"But we'd have so much fun," said Leon.

Noel stared down at him and couldn't tell from his twin's gleaming eyes whether Leon was serious or not.

"Keep working," said Leon.

When Noel fitted the last stone in place, he wiped the sweat from his face with his arm and helped Leon plaster it with mud.

They finished by the time the torch was guttering low. For a moment they stared at their handiwork, and the only sound was their heavy breathing. Noel picked up the empty pail. He was smeared with mud up to his elbows, and the passageway stank of sweat and urgency.

"You realize," he said softly, "that the only way out now is the way they'll be coming in."

Leon gave his one-sided shrug. "We'll make it. I told you I have this thing figured out."

A screech of rage reverberated through the passageway. Noel whirled around and lifted the wooden bucket in self-defense. Leon swung the torch so fast he nearly put it out. Noel could see nothing. His heart was racing. Adrenaline pumped him; he was ready to fight, to run, to do something to get out of here.

"Mondoun," he whispered.

"No!" whispered Leon back. "An animal maybe—"

Something flew at them. Noel fended it off with the bucket, and deflected, it fell to the ground with a soft thud. It was a bird carcass, decapitated, the blood still fresh on the feathers. Tied to it was a thing of bone and fur and clay.

The screech came again, echoing from all directions.

Noel and Leon drew involuntarily closer together. Leon's face had lost its reckless confidence. Noel didn't feel too confident himself.

"I told you it was Mondoun," he said.

"How does it feel to be right all the time?" retorted Leon. He pulled out his dagger. "Maybe we should—"

The zombies appeared in the passageway, two shambling, slack-faced figures. Noel knocked one down with the bucket, and Leon dispatched the other with the dagger. He glanced at Noel.

"Move out of the way."

Noel gripped his bucket harder. He listened, knowing that it was far from over. "You don't have to kill him in cold blood."

"Cold or hot, the result is the same," said Leon indifferently.

"They aren't our enemies."

Leon shoved him aside and sank the dagger deep into the second zombie. "Now we don't have to worry about them again."

"You—"

The bats came in a sudden flurry, swooping through the passageway in a dark cloud of furry bodies, tiny fangs glistening, eyes gleaming red in the torchlight, their leathery wings whipping the air.

Noel and Leon ducked as the bats streamed overhead. Noel quivered, trying to master his rising tide of revulsion. But ever since he'd first been attacked by the vampire bats in the jungle, he hadn't been able to react rationally. Now he huddled on the ground, his heart whamming against his rib cage, his eyes squeezed shut, his fingers clutching the bucket so hard they hurt.

The bats passed over them and streamed on to the end of the passageway. Blocked, they doubled back. Now their high-pitched chittering and squeaks seemed more frenzied as though they were being driven by some unseen force. They swooped low over Noel and Leon. Noel felt one drop on to his shoulder, felt the scrabbling claws clutch.

With a scream, he fought his way up, only to be engulfed in their midst. Furry bodies milled about him, brushing his face, squeaking in his ears, thudding against his back and chest. He breathed in the musty scent of their fur, and swung the bucket around him frantically. He managed to hit several of them.

Some lay stunned; others struggled feebly to move, to fly.

Leon sprang to his feet. "Let's get out of this!"

He plunged ahead, using the dying torch to sear them. Noel followed, choked and desperate. He swung the bucket wildly but most of them veered away from it this time. Some, however, got entangled with each other. They squeaked furiously and fought each other.

"I see daylight ahead!" shouted Noel.

He plunged ahead of Leon, hearing his twin say something but not paying any heed.

The closer to the light he drew, the more the bats lagged behind. Then he was clear of them, panting and feeling filthy from their contact. Blood ran down his cheek from a scratch. He wiped at it and quickened his pace to a run.

Forgetting the need for caution, he bolted outside into the dazzling sunlight, stumbled on the sloping hillside and nearly lost his footing. Scrambling, he caught his balance and paused.

Only then did he see Mondoun standing there, his ebony skin gleaming in the sun as though oiled, his head shaved, his eyes burning fiercely. Behind the *Bocor* stood a cluster of perhaps twenty pirates. Black Lonigan, bearded and earringed, his meaty hands clutching a sword, waited at their head. His dark eyes held a stony threat that made Noel swallow hard.

"Flush out the other whoreson," said Lonigan.

Mondoun lifted his long arms, but before he could start an incantation, Leon came out on his own and joined Noel.

"I have delivered them to you," said Mondoun. "These defilers of the sacred rites have displeased the gods—"

"Later. Ye can have them when I'm done," said Lonigan.

"Give me their hearts," said Mondoun. He reached out with a long crimson feather and touched the left side of Noel's chest and the right side of Leon's. "Twin hearts, cut from living flesh. And a measure of their blood."

"When I'm done, damn ye!" roared Lonigan. "Now, ye pair of mangy swabbies, where be the women and the boy?"

"Drowned," said Noel, meeting his eyes.

"Lies!" shrieked Mondoun. "They live. Believe not these tricksters, who have betrayed you even more than you know."

Lonigan cast him an impatient glance. "What's this?"

"Uh, he's just babbling," said Noel hastily. "It's true that they drowned. I can show you Lady Pamela's grave."

As he spoke he was aware of Leon shifting his weight. Noel dared not glance away from Lonigan, but from his peripheral vision he could see that Leon had removed his sling. He held his left arm as though his wound hurt him, but Noel was aware of the dagger hidden at Leon's side.

Use it, thought Noel. *Right through Lonigan's heart.*

"What about the other one?" demanded Lonigan fiercely. "If the governor's wife—"

"Yes," said Noel firmly. "There was no need for those women to be abandoned like that on a disabled ship in a hurricane."

"Hurricane?" shouted Lonigan. "Bah! Ye fool, that were just a wee storm."

"Then why did you sail so hurriedly to escape it? Why did you abandon your prisoners to drown along with the slave cargo and all the other—"

"Silence! His tongue is a deceiving one," said Mondoun. "The boy lives. The woman lives. Why not ask him what he does here in the caves—"

Leon threw the dagger, and the weapon struck Baba Mondoun squarely in the throat. Blood spurted, and the *Bocor*'s hands raked the air frantically as though he meant to pull it out. Then he toppled to the ground and lay still.

As though on cue, dark clouds rolled across the sun and the jungle grew unnaturally still. The black pirates moaned, but a harsh command from Lonigan silenced them. Drawing his brace of pistols, he pulled back the hammers and pointed them at Noel and Leon.

"Good throw," murmured Noel. "Wrong target."

Leon had turned pale and was leaning over as though he'd pulled his wound again. But he still managed to glare at Noel. "What do you mean? He was about to—"

"He means, matey," said Lonigan's booming voice, "that with me lyin' there dead ye could have outsmarted the rest of this scurvy lot. But killin' Baba, ah, now, that was a piece of bad manners we won't forgive. Will we, lads?"

They roared and surged up to surround Noel and Leon. Noel kicked and punched, but he was overpowered and soon found his hands tied behind his back. Leon was also trussed without regard for his injury.

Lonigan poked Baba's body with his toe. "Shame. I'll have to find me another laddie of the dark ways."

"Why?" said Noel in bewilderment.

"To keep me legend fearsome, of course," said Lonigan. "There be no one else who dares put in at this island with Baba Mondoun guarding me treasure. He did make a wondrous good curse. Natty, you and Tate go find the woman and boy. The rest of ye take these two lubbers down and put 'em aboard. We'll have our fun with 'em later."

The captain sheathed his sword and rubbed his hands together. "I've got to count me treasure. Get on with the lot of ye and let me be."

Natty Gumbel cackled and gave Noel a shove that started him walking. Noel glanced at Leon. "You know what's going to happen when he finds—"

"It *will* work. We still have our bargaining point."

Noel sighed. "Oh, yeah? And what if he runs us through before we get to bargain? Have you considered that?"

Leon glanced at him, then dropped his gaze. "Don't depress me."

CHAPTER 12

Noel's head was throbbing through the temples. It felt like it had been stuffed with wool, overstuffed in fact, for it was nearly bursting. Pressure roared in his ears. He yawned, making his jaw crack, but that didn't alleviate the discomfort. He squinted open his eyes, saw the deck shifting beneath him, and closed them quickly.

At the moment life was not good. He was hanging upside down; the ropes lashed around his ankles were digging too tightly into his skin; and too much blood had pooled in his head.

He curled his abdominal muscles a bit to lift his head, and the change of position helped enormously. It also enabled him to see Lady Mountleigh and Neddie sitting huddled on a stack of coiled rope in the bow of the brigantine. Kona and three more escaped slaves found hiding in the jungle stood in chains. Leon, stripped to the waist, was being tied to the mast while Black Lonigan shook out the weighted cords of a cat-o'-nine-tails.

"It's Moses' punishment fer ye, matey, if ye don't talk now," roared Lonigan. "Forty stripes less one, and I promise ye they'll each and every one hurt like Judgment Day." He whipped the cat across Leon's back. "There's the first, aye, ye scoundrel. Now where's me treasure, eh?"

Leon gasped against the mast and made no answer. The cat struck again, crisscrossing his back with red welts. Nearby, hanging upside down from an iron hook like a marlin caught for a fishing contest, Noel winced in sympathy.

He had finally realized that Leon was affecting Lonigan's mind so that the pirate hadn't seen through their trick in the cave. Otherwise the man would surely have noticed the still wet mud walling up the passageway. He should have connected that to the mud smeared on both Leon and Noel and the wooden pail Noel had been carrying when they'd been captured. But the whole flimsy ruse had fooled him, so he had to be under some kind of mental control from Leon.

Which exasperated Noel all the more. If Leon could do this much, why couldn't he persuade Lonigan to let them go? Why couldn't he convince the pirates that their prisoners didn't exist at all?

Of course, to be fair, Noel knew that Leon's gift didn't always work. Leon wasn't very skilled at using his ability. Sometimes he was too forceful and damaged his victims; sometimes he had no effect at all.

Still, remaining stubbornly silent wasn't doing any of them good.

Another lash cracked out. Leon yelped that time. Listening, Noel frowned with reluctant sympathy. He himself had been flogged before. In other circumstances he might have felt that Leon deserved what he was getting. Right now, it brought back unwelcome memories of agonizing pain, of the sobs for mercy that couldn't be uttered, of the rage and the humiliation, of the dreadful wait through the seconds between each blow.

The next time Leon screamed. The pirates cheered and started laying bets on how long Leon would last before he begged for mercy.

Noel hadn't expected him to last this long. Leon's greed must be stronger than he'd realized.

But the deal between Noel and Leon had been that they would hide the treasure to use as a bargaining point with the pirates, not that they would die rather than give it up.

Noel said, "I'll tell you where it is."

Lonigan's head swiveled around. "Eh? What's that?"

"I said I'll tell you where it is."

Leon raised his head. His face was wet from tears and sweat. "No!"

"By God, at last!" roared Lonigan. He flung down the cat and strode over to Noel. "Cut this piece of cod fodder down."

Natty Gumbel and another pirate lowered Noel to the deck with a thud that wrenched a grunt from him. Gumbel's foot rolled Noel over onto his stomach. The cold steel of a dagger slid between Noel's wrists. There was a brief tug on the rope, then Noel's hands were free. His swollen arms fell like lead casings on either side of him.

Gumbel kicked him. "Get up, then! God's my witness, but ye've made things sorry fer yerself, ye have."

Noel dragged himself upright and swayed under a bout of dizziness. The blood drained through him, and he felt strangely light-headed. He glanced at Gumbel, who glared at him with one sightless eye staring out to port, then faced Lonigan.

The pirate captain towered over Noel, and the scowl on his bearded face was thunderous indeed. "Now," he said. His meaty paw gripped Noel's shoulder and pulled Noel up to his tiptoes. "Ye've got one chance to tell me what ye've done with it, or I'll slit yer gullet and feed you to the fishes. So help me God I will!"

Noel looked into the man's eyes and believed him. Feeling a little short of breath Noel replied, "One condition."

Lonigan's eyes widened, and he shook Noel fiercely. "What?" he bellowed. "Who the hell said anything about conditions? I'll not have any of yer bloody conditions, nay, and be damned to ye!"

"Then you won't have your treasure," said Noel.

Lonigan put his face so close to Noel's that Noel could feel the man's hot breath. It stank of tobacco and rum. "Yer playin' with fire, me lad," he said softly. "I can have yer eyes took out and yer tongue slit. I can cut off yer ears, aye, and maybe a foot. How would ye like to spend the rest of yer days hobblin' about Tortuga as a charity beggar, eh? I can have O'Malley there stitch ye into a sail with a dab of iron on yer leg and put ye overboard like a kitten in a sack. I can put ye on a hook and drag ye in our wake fer shark bait. Eh? Which do ye like, lad?"

"I don't want to die, and I don't want to be tortured," said Noel, forcing himself to meet the man's gaze although he was afraid of showing his fear. "I'll tell you where the treasure is if you'll meet my condition."

Lonigan shoved Noel away so hard he went staggering. "Yer in no position to bargain with me!"

Noel took a deep breath. "Then you won't find it, ever. You can spend the rest of your life searching this island but you won't see your gold again."

Lonigan's broad nostrils flared. His eyes bulged. His face turned red, then purple. With a roar, he charged, gripping Noel around the throat and driving him bodily back against the railing. "Ye lily-livered, conniving, pox-ridden scrap of vermin! I'll teach ye to make threats against Black Lonigan. By God I will!"

Noel struggled, but his air was already choked off. The pressure on his throat mounted. Black dots swam before his eyes. He reached out blindly, choking, and felt his lungs convulse for air.

With the last bit of strength left to him, he whispered hoarsely, "Let . . . woman and . . . boy . . . go."

Across the deck, Leon called, "You'll never find it if you kill us!"

Lonigan roared again, shaking his big head like an enraged bull. But just as Noel felt the world sag out from beneath him, Lonigan released him. Noel dropped to his knees and gulped in sweet air, deep lungfuls of it. His throat ached so much he felt he would never talk again.

But he had to. He couldn't trust Leon to finish making the bargain. Lady Mountleigh had to survive in order for history to remain intact. If he died today, his presence in this century would make no dent on events. If he lived, he would spend the rest of his life exiled in solitude on this island, so that he would not affect others. Somehow, he had to contrive it so that Leon would do the same.

But survival was by no means certain yet. Rubbing his throat, Noel looked up at Lonigan and slowly climbed to his feet. His LOC felt slightly warm on his wrist as though it was activating.

He glanced at it, and saw with disappointment that it remained black and dead on his wrist. The sensation must be due to his returning circulation.

"What good is the woman to you?" he rasped out, his voice still hoarse. "Let them go."

"Are ye her gallant then?" asked Lonigan in plain bewilderment.

"No."

"Are ye her kinsman?"

Noel started to shake his head, then said, "I am responsible for her safety."

Lonigan narrowed his eyes. "It's plain to see yer a naive man with little knowledge of the world. Governor Mountleigh has been in office a year, and already he's made of himself a sore trial for the Brotherhood. He's barred us from Port Royal. He sends those damned naval sloops out like wolf packs to hunt us down and keep us from a good living. Bah! It be time and above that the man learned a lesson. If he wants his lady and his heir returned safe and sound to his bosom, then he'll have to meet *our* conditions."

Noel didn't blink. "Which would you rather have? Access to Port Royal, or your loot already stockpiled?"

Lonigan reached for him again. "By God, ye dog! It's my treasure and I'll not have ye keeping it from me!"

"But you can't find it, remember?" said Noel. He held Lonigan's baffled gaze a moment, then added with steel in his voice, "Let the woman and child go. Put them safely ashore with provisions, and I'll return your treasure."

"Yer mad. How can I trust ye?"

"How am I to trust *you*?" replied Noel evenly. He knew Lonigan was wavering. The man stood with his powerful shoulders hunched and his head lowered.

"And what's fer yerself out of this?" asked Lonigan finally.

"Sail ho!" came the cry from the crow's nest before Noel could answer.

Lonigan whipped around and rushed to the starboard railing with his spyglass. "God's bones!" he shouted. "They're barely a quarter of a mile off shore. Are ye daft to let them sneak up on us so close?"

"The sun's goin' down, Captain," came the lookout's aggrieved voice. "I couldn't see."

"Couldn't see," fumed Lonigan. "I'll make ye think ye can't see when I dig out yer eyeballs! What flag, damn ye!"

"British."

"Beat to quarters!" came the cry.

The pirates snapped to action, changing instantly from a mob of hoodlums to an efficient, well-trained crew. One of the musicians pulled out a drum and began pounding on it. The pirates scurried into the rigging. Others turned the windlass and brought up the anchor.

"Dammit, faster!" roared Lonigan. "We're caught in harbor with our pants down. A pretty pigeon we are. Unfurl sail! Hard about!"

The other ship came at them under full canvas, fast and closing with every passing minute. The *Medusa* turned ponderously, her sails luffing before they finally caught the wind. The brigantine headed toward the mouth of the little harbor, gliding past the half-submerged wreckage of her sister ship.

"It's a sloop," said Natty Gumbel, crowding the rail beside Noel. He tugged a line taut and dallied it around a belaying pin with deft hands. "We can outgun her."

Another hail came from the lookout. "Another ship!"

"Full sail!" shouted Lonigan. He ran to the helmsman and cursed him roundly. "Damn the course. Tate! Harley! Crowd on more sail!"

"We can't outrun her, Captain," said the helmsman.

Already Noel could see the sloop changing direction to intersect their path. She was a graceful thing, her simple lines gliding over the waves under the spread of her canvas. A puff of smoke suddenly wreathed her side. Moments later, Noel heard the faint boom of a cannon. The ball crashed harmlessly into the water more than five hundred yards off their prow. It was intended as a warning.

"Pass word to the gunner's mate," said Lonigan grimly.

A man scurried below. Along the sides of the *Medusa,* portholes opened and cannons were run out, making the lower deck rumble ominously beneath Noel's feet.

"We dare not take on the British Navy," said the sailing master. "Were it Dutch we faced or even the damned Frenchies, aye, then we should fight. But—"

"Where's yer courage, man?" retorted Lonigan scathingly. "Do ye mean we should surrender to those dogs? Never! I'll not hang from England's gibbet."

He whipped out his cutlass and swung it wildly to send his men scattering. "Natty!" he said and pointed at Noel. "Take that dog below and chain him where he'll cause no mischief. I'll deal with him later."

"Aye," said Gumbel. He glared at Noel with his good eye and gave Noel a shove. "On with ye."

Reluctantly Noel obeyed. He didn't want to be trapped below in the stinking hold. He had the unpleasant suspicion that in battle cannonballs would probably come crashing through the hull and land in his lap. He would much rather be topside, where he could see the action. But Gumbel jabbed him in the back with a pistol, and Noel climbed down the ladder.

The activity below decks was as hectic as up in the rigging. The gunnery crews were busy with measuring out gunpowder, cutting fuses, tamping in wads of cloth, and loading shot. A scrawny boy stood ready with a burning torch in his hand. At the signal he would run down the row of waiting cannons and light the fuses in rapid succession.

Noel tensed and slowed his pace. He had to try something, and an idea was coming to him.

Gumbel jabbed him in the back. "Get on! Here's no place to be gawkin'."

At the end of the row, Noel gauged the distance between him and the boy with the torch. The gun crews had finished loading and were rolling the heavy weapons forward. "Aim high," said the gunner's mate, squinting out a porthole and working out trajectory figures. "There's no sayin' we'll wait until the range is good."

Noel went into action. He jumped forward, then whirled on Gumbel with a boxer's kick that knocked Gumbel's wrist aside just as the pistol fired. The ball whined past Noel and imbedded itself in a wooden bulkhead. The torch boy ducked involuntarily and nearly set a keg of powder aflame. While the men were yelling at him, Noel seized him and wrested the torch from his hand.

"Get him!" yelled Gumbel.

Noel knocked Gumbel aside with his shoulder and ran down the row, lighting the fuses over the howling protests of the crews. Men scattered, and the cannons belched forth their thunder. The violent recoil of the guns was something Noel hadn't counted on. He leapt aside just in time to avoid being crushed as a twelve-pounder came rolling back on its cart and crashed into the blocks. Gumbel, who'd been reaching for him, was less lucky. The cannon knocked him down and rolled over his leg. There was a spurt of blood and Gumbel writhed, screaming.

For Noel, there was nowhere to run. The others were on him now, pummeling him to the deck that was gritty with gunpowder. The torch fell from his hand, and fire blazed down a trail of spilled powder, heading quicker than thought toward the pile of kegs.

"God have mercy!" yelled someone in horror.

Noel himself tried to get to his feet and run, but he wasn't fast enough. No one was fast enough although some of the men reached the ladder and tried to climb it.

The explosion blew out the starboard side of the ship with a crimson and orange fireball and a mighty gush of black smoke. Debris rained down, and with a groan the ship listed heavily to the right, going down already into the clear green waters.

Knocked bodily into a bulkhead rib on the opposite side of the ship, Noel came to in a daze. Blood was dripping into his eye from a gash in his forehead. He touched the cut numbly, unable to feel any pain from it. His ears were ringing, and he couldn't quite pull himself together.

"We're sinking!" screamed someone.

"Where's the surgeon!" shouted someone else.

Groans and cries of pain rose. To Noel they sounded far, far away. He shook his head in an effort to clear it. There was something important that he needed to do. If only he could remember what it was.

A dark shape appeared in the gloom and smoke. It knelt beside Noel, who had managed to sit up.

"Hurry, bwana," said Kona. Concerned and bleeding from numerous minor abrasions, he patted Noel's shoulder and tugged. "Get up. Hurry fast."

Noel climbed to his feet and staggered to the ladder. Kona shoved him to get him started and Noel finally made it topside.

Up here, smoke boiled from the burning guts of the ship. Part of the deck was gone, leaving a jagged edge that seemed somehow unreal. The ship was listing badly to that side. A shudder went through her. Screams came from everywhere.

Noel's wits returned. He looked around and saw Leon still tied to the mast. Plucking a dagger from the slack hand of a dead man, Noel handed it to Kona. "Cut Leon free."

Kona shook his head. "Save good bwana. Not bad one."

"Cut him free!" commanded Noel and plunged into the smoke in search of Lady Mountleigh.

He found her lying on the deck with a terrified Neddie at her side. For a moment Noel thought she was dead, but she had only swooned. Little sparks had burned holes in her dress. Noel beat on the places that were smoldering, and slung her limp form over his shoulder.

"Neddie, come!" he said sharply.

He held out his hand, and Neddie took it without hesitation. The boy's eyes were wide and vacant. He seemed to be in shock.

The survivors of the blast were climbing overboard. Two dinghies had been broken out, but they weren't big enough to hold all the men. Fighting broke out for one, with swimmers pulling passengers out and climbing in themselves.

Noel stared at the debris-strewn water and knew he couldn't get both the woman and child to shore. Kona joined him at the railing and looked over dubiously.

"Kona no swim good. Too far from ground."

The sloop was coming up now. They were hailed, and Noel waved.

"I have a woman and child!" he yelled. "Can you take them aboard first?"

"Aye! Do you surrender?"

Noel snorted. "Yes, yes. Just come on before we sink!"

The firm, aristocratic tones of the British officer carried clearly across the water. "Everyone form orderly lines. Put down your weapons. If you resist capture you will be shot."

The pirates were too shaken to resist. Noel glanced around for Leon, but his twin wasn't in sight. He faced Kona with sudden suspicion.

The African youth's face held a stony expression. Only his eyes betrayed his despair. "Kona is slave again. Kona always slave."

"No," said Noel with such vehemence, Kona looked at him. "No, you will not always be a slave. You are destined for an important role someday. Your name will be remembered in history. Even the white bwanas will know of you and your deeds."

Kona's eyes gathered in the hope Noel offered and brightened for a moment before they grew dull again.

"Listen to me," said Noel urgently. His LOC was growing even hotter on his wrist, searing hot, so hot he slipped his fingers beneath it to take it off. Then he didn't in the importance of what he was trying to communicate to Kona. "You must never give up your dream of freedom. You must share that dream with others. You must give hope where you can."

"Is hard."

Noel gripped his bony shoulder for a moment. "I know. I wish I could help you."

A seaman in clean duck trousers and a pigtail climbed up over the railing. "Lumme! You've 'ad quite a knock to your pate, ain't you?" He chucked Neddie under the chin and reached for Lady Mountleigh. "Cor, she's a bit of an armful, ain't she? Better made than my Belle, back 'ome."

"Treat her with respect," said Noel sharply. "She's Lady Mountleigh, and this is her son."

The seaman paled. "Mountleigh! Not Governor—"

"Yes," said Noel.

The man gulped. Leaning over the railing, he yelled, "Look sharp, mates! This 'ere's the governor's own lady and 'is tyke."

While the seamen lowered Lady Mountleigh tenderly over the side and passed her by careful degrees down to a waiting dinghy, Kona's gaze shifted. Noel looked too and saw a second ship coming up on the starboard side, opposite the sloop. There was something odd about her. Something he couldn't quite put his finger on.

Then he saw her outlines shimmer, just for a moment, and his heart stopped. He stared, feeling as though his head had detached itself from his body and was floating away. It couldn't be. It wasn't possible.

He took a step toward her, then stopped. The rest of his surroundings seemed to fade. He could gaze only at the ship, at the hugeness of her, of the splendid height of her tall masts. She was from another era, he realized. Her lines were more refined. She had more decks, a different style of poop; her sails were of a different cut. She was ghostly white, with a pearly, iridescent shimmer to her sails as though they had been fashioned of parachute silk. The huge, blazing sun setting behind her played hues of plum, coral, and yellow across her bows, yet she seemed almost transparent in places, as though made of spun glass.

He realized with amazement that she was sitting on top of the water, rather than in it. Noel gripped himself, wanting to believe, yet not daring to. He didn't understand how it could be here, how they could have done it. He didn't quite want to let hope rise, not yet.

Yet a figure appeared on that ghostly deck. It waved, and there was something familiar in the stance and the set of those broad shoulders. Noel took a few more steps forward, heedless of the listing deck beneath his feet. Yes, he could see now. A big man with bushy red hair and a broad grin on his face. He waved again. No, he was beckoning.

Noel's vision blurred with sudden tears. It was Trojan Heitz, his colleague and best friend. Trojan's specialty was medieval history. Independently wealthy, he worked for the Time Institute as a hobby more than an avocation. But beneath his casual demeanor, he was just as serious about history and its preservation as anyone else.

Noel swallowed, unable to trust his eyes. Trojan couldn't be here. It had to be a figment of his imagination; maybe he had a concussion and was suffering a delirious hallucination. Two travelers could not enter the same time stream concurrently. It was one of the laws of interdimensional travel. So how . . .

"Mother of God," whispered someone behind Noel. "A ghost ship come to claim the dead."

"Come to collect Black Lonigan's soul, most like," said another, "and take it down to hell. He would mess about with black magic and such."

The LOC on Noel's wrist burned as hot as ever. It flickered fitfully as though trying to activate.

"Noel . . ." came Trojan's voice, so faint Noel almost couldn't hear it. "Hurry. Come through. . . ."

He saw a shimmering gangplank run out. The ghost ship drew closer and closer until it almost brushed the sinking *Medusa*. Noel walked toward it, his heart hammering wildly, his throat so choked with emotion it hurt.

Then a movement from the corner of his eye caught his attention. He turned and saw Leon, poised for flight near the skewed bit of railing left on this side of the ship. The wind was blowing Leon's black hair. His chin was up, his eyes unreadable at that distance.

Noel beckoned to him.

Leon shook his head.

"Noel . . ." called Trojan's voice, fainter than ever, so diminished now Noel almost imagined he heard the words. "Come now . . . or never. . . ."

He could not wait. Noel stepped forward and reached out to the gangplank. Although it looked completely insubstantial, he felt something solid. Climbing onto it, he crossed the distance between the two ships. For a moment he felt the ghost ship yaw in the waves, then he was dissolving into a gray mist as familiar and as comforting as home, as gentle a return as his departure had been violent.

Centuries later, he materialized on the platform in Laboratory 14, disoriented, slightly nauseated from the side effects of travel, dazzled by the glare of lights and the sea of faces.

He swayed and took a step, staggered and sank to his knees. He was crying, he realized with embarrassment, crying in front of everyone. Yet another part of him did not care because of the relief and gratitude surging through him. They hadn't abandoned him. They had brought him back. Somehow, although he did not understand, they brought him back.

He couldn't quite focus, couldn't quite make out the words babbling around him. He tried to stand but failed, then Trojan's voice came through clearly and Trojan's hands helped him up.

"Noel, it's all right. You're back. You're back with us."

Noel looked into Trojan's blue eyes, misty now and full of affection. Only then did Noel believe it had finally happened. With a gasp, he hugged Trojan tightly and was nearly crushed in return. Trojan thumped him heavily on the back.

"We thought for a while that we'd lost you for good," he said, his voice hoarse with emotion. "Don't scare us like that again."

Noel grinned and looked around at the technicians and historians gathered there. Even Dr. Rugle was wiping her eyes, and he'd never suspected the old hag herself of owning tear ducts before.

Shakily he wiped his face. "How—how long was I gone?"

Trojan's expression sobered. "Seven days, present elapsed time. One hundred sixty-eight hours—"

"—and twenty-four minutes," broke in Bruthe, the senior travel technician.

Everyone laughed nervously.

Trojan glared at Bruthe and said to Noel, "That's as fast as we could get the programming in place for a manual return. The *Flying Dutchman* was my idea. Not bad, do you think?"

Noel grinned. "Not bad at all." He pulled the coin from his pocket and flipped it at Trojan. "Here, have a piece of eight."

Trojan caught the coin with a gasp of delight, which he swiftly muffled. He glanced furtively at Dr. Rugle, who was frowning, and closed his fingers over the coin.

"I don't think—"

"Whoa, Dr. Rugle," broke in Noel with a swagger. "I've got more souvenirs to pass around. This is for you." He pulled out the pearl necklace and in stunned silence she took it.

The others crowded around to look at it.

"Genuine pearls."

"Fabulous size. Perfectly matched."

"Lovely."

"Yes, er, lovely," said Dr. Rugle, clearing her throat. "But quite against regulations—"

"Are you going to make me take them back?" asked Noel.

Everyone laughed, and Dr. Rugle softened. "I suppose not."

Noel grinned at her, then a wave of dizziness passed over him. The next thing he heard was Dr. Rugle's gruff voice giving orders.

"Everyone clear back. Let the medical staff through. He's got to be examined now. Stand back, please. Kedran, may I extend to you a warm welcome back. I am pleased that you adhered to your oath and did not alter history. Your methods were perhaps a bit unorthodox; however, we need not go into that now. Naturally the staff will want to run extensive tests on you. In the meantime, we'll process the LOC recordings. When you are released from the infirmary, I shall want to see you in my office for debriefings. No one has ever been in the time stream this long before. We have much to do."

Noel stared at her and struggled to find a retort. Even pearls weren't going to keep the old bat from making her speeches. But before the words came to him, Trojan's hand gripped his with a warning squeeze. Noel relaxed. It was just like old times—him losing his temper and Trojan cooling him down.

He smiled at his friend, then the medical team was there.

"Got to get this LOC off while leaving you some hide," said one doctor, a rather pretty blonde he hadn't seen before. He regretted not saving the pearls for her. "It's practically fused to your skin."

Noel smiled at her and held up his left wrist to show the burn mark. "I peeled it off when it went haywire the first time."

"Good thing you put it back on," said Trojan, who refused to leave when Dr. Rugle shooed everyone else away. "Without it we couldn't have traced you at all."

"It worked for a while, then it quit." Noel frowned, remembering the panic he'd felt. "It just *quit*."

The pretty doctor glanced up sharply and gave him a shot.

Trojan patted his shoulder. "Of course it quit. We turned it off so that we could link it to our return program signal. What did you think?"

Noel wanted to tell him about the voodoo and strange messages from the *Bocor* coming in over the LOC's transmitter, but he was starting to drift from the medication and it seemed too much trouble right now. His eyes felt heavy, but before he succumbed to the fuzziness there was something he had to tell Trojan . . . something important.

"Mr. Heitz," said Bruthe with a queer note to his voice. "Is that LOC deactivated yet? I'm still getting a wave pattern in the time stream."

Noel forced open his eyes, and for a moment the fuzziness of the drug receded. "It's him," he said.

"Who?" said Trojan. "What are you talking about?"

"Not now," said the doctor impatiently. "I want this man taken down to the infirmary so I can remove this fused piece of equipment under a sterile field."

"Wait," said Noel.

He lifted his head and saw with irritation that at some point he'd been strapped to a gurney. When? He didn't remember.

"It's probably that ghost pattern we kept picking up," said Bruthe. "I thought the system would clear when Mr. Kedran came back."

Noel frowned, momentarily distracted. Since when had Bruthe started tacking respectful misters to people's names?

Did the attitude seem different around here? He was drifting again. He blinked, forcing himself to stay focused.

"Have to tell you about him," he said.

"Who?" repeated Trojan. "Take it easy, Noel. There's no rush."

"The drug's taking hold," said the doctor.

"Leon Nardek," said Noel. He let the name hang in the air for a moment while he stared up into Trojan's puzzled eyes. He saw his friend sort it out. Trojan blinked. He opened his mouth.

"Yes," said Noel. "A double, created in the time stream anomaly when I first went through. He wouldn't come back with me."

Bruthe grunted. "Would have been impossible. It was set for your pattern only."

"He's my double."

"Reversed maybe. The wave is moving backward."

Noel glowered in rising irritation. "Of course reversed," he snapped, ignoring the doctor who was taking his pulse. "I'm left-handed. He's right-handed. His heart's on the right side. His name is the reverse of mine. Even his personality is . . ."

He stopped, unable to go on explaining.

Trojan gripped his shoulder. "There's plenty of time, my friend. We don't have to deal with the problem now. If he's an anomaly, chances are he'll fade soon from the time stream. Right, Bruthe?"

"Hmm?" said the technician absently. "Oh, right. Probably. No, I'm sure he will. He has to. What's to support him? It's not like he's an original. He'll fade all right."

"Monitor it anyway," said Trojan.

"Look, Heitz, I'll do my job."

Noel closed his eyes and let them roll him away. In his mind's eye he conjured up a picture of Leon . . . a fraction shorter, his eyes a lighter shade of gray, his jawline more blurred. He saw Leon smirking, Leon plotting mischief, Leon groveling with fear. He heard that triumphant note in Leon's voice when his duplicate had said the link between them was broken and he was no longer Noel's shadow.

Maybe he would fade away soon from the time stream. Shadows couldn't exist, after all, without their originator. But if Leon had told the truth, then he would continue in the time stream, creating havoc, upsetting history, unraveling the future.

Had Leon told the truth? Could Leon tell the truth?

Lying was his nature. He'd love leaving Noel to wonder for the rest of eternity.

As Noel wondered now.